The Magdalene Diaries

Other Books by Robert J. Grant
(Non–Fiction)

Love and Roses from David

Edgar Cayce on Angels, Archangels, and the Unseen Forces

The Place We Call Home

Universe of Worlds

The Magdalene Diaries

By Robert J. Grant

A.R.E. Press • Virginia Beach • Virginia

A.R.E. Press
215 67th Street
Virginia Beach, VA 23451-2061

Library of Congress Cataloguing-in-Publication Data
Grant, Robert J.
    The Magdalene diaries / by Robert J. Grant
        p.   cm.
    ISBN 0-87604-504-2 (trade pbk.)
    1. Mary Magdalene, Saint–Fiction. 2. Bible. N.T.–History of Biblical events–Fiction. 3. Christian women saints–Fiction. 4. Palestine–Fiction.
I. Title.
    PS3607.R365M34 2005
    813'.6—dc22

                                    2005018215

Cover design by Richard Boyle

*For Chet Winney, and
John and Jim Grant*

CONTENTS

1

When Dawn Came—
In the Dark Night of My Soul

I remember the day I died. I remember the day I was born— or re–born as this woman who writes these words. From this place I am now hiding, I will try to write all that I experienced, all that I witnessed—the glorious days and nights . . . when God came down to earth and walked among us as a man.

My time is short, I know, to tell the stories of this man Jesus (known among the Nazarenes as Jesus ben Joseph) that no doubt many will not believe—it will seem too incredible to be true, but it was. Incredible. And it was, and is, true. All that I write here—from my heart—is true.

Let me tell you why I must write in haste. You see, the Romans are searching for me—and others like me—the others who loved and followed this man, Jesus, and when they find me, my life will be over. How strange it is that one man can topple an empire as great as Rome. But he did. He set the souls of so many free through a simple but profound teaching: Jesus taught us that God is a God of Spirit, and dwells within the heart of everyone—man, woman, and child. He taught us that we are *the children of God, beloved and eternal.* How many times did he say, "Where two or more of you gather together, there is God in the midst of you"? So many times. And now, those who loved him are a direct threat to the Romans, who seek to rule by force, tyranny, and if there be religion or worship it is to be done under their direction—that we go to dead temples and pay alms to dead gods. Yes, they would kill me even for writing these words. This man, Jesus, taught me that there is an eternal flame of spirit alive and vibrant within my heart—that is *at one* with God. When he said that to me, I not only believed, but I knew—I knew in my heart it was true. It was like I was blind before I met him, and after . . . I could see. See more clearly than I've ever seen before.

So I bore witness, I was there, and was with Jesus everywhere—and they know my face, all too well, I am afraid—so I must write as much as quickly as I can—day and night if needs be—to leave the record behind and pray that someone finds it. I fear not death, for I know it is only like the passing of the spring to the summer. This is another truth Jesus gave to me. From here onward, I will call him the Master. Though I knew him and was privileged to call him friend, he was the perfect manifestation of God and man. He was . . . he is . . . the Master.

My only fear at this time is that there will not be time for me to write of all that he did, and said, all that he promised to me and to the generations to come. I will try. Even now, I can feel his presence, and I know that there will be time for me to finish what he has ordained me to do. In the echoes of my mind I can hear, "Write, Mary, write . . . have no fear for I am with you now, and always, even unto the end of this life, and into the beginning of the next."

Yes. I will Master. I will. Even here in the darkness, of this subterranean hiding place, an oil lamp upon the stone table, where I write, I can feel *Him*, and He assures me that there is time for me to write what I know—to write of what I saw Him do, tell of what he said. I know my fate and it isn't long. I will be hunted down like the others, and killed no doubt. The cost of following the Master is high, in worldly standards.

For, he told all of us, those of us who chose the rituals of love instead of blood sacrifice: "If they came after me, they will come after you. But do not be afraid—for I went before you—and I will be with you always—all days—especially the hard days, even unto the end of this physical life. But I will lift you up from out of this physical shell and take you where I *am*—to a sacred, beautiful place where you will not remember the pain, only the love . . . only the love."

I hold onto those words, now. Because this human frail self—the self known by the name of Mary of Magdalene, is afraid. I've never died before, and I fear the pain that comes before death. Forgive me, Master. I'm as afraid as you were in that terrible night in the garden of Gethsemane—before they hunted you down. Even so, I can sense or feel that even now, he smiles. Although he was put to death by the Romans by the cruel crucifixion, before he took his last breath, he smiled upon all of us who gathered around him—he smiled. Smiled! In that terrible place of the skull—Golgotha, and said, "This too shall pass. Soon you shall see me again. And all will be well."

His words were true. He walks among us still. What God has ordained, nothing can halt. And God ordained that one day man would overcome death. And Jesus, the Master, did overcome death. At the time of his death, I mourned greatly. I did not understand, but I do now. Forgive me my friends, my foes, I am getting ahead of myself, I will begin at the beginning of when my own life was changed by the Master. You see, he saved me from death. That is where all of this begins—with the death of my old self, and the birth of this woman who now writes here in this secret place.

Those of the Sanhedrin, those of the so-called church of our day, despised me long before the Master came into our midst. For they saw me as a woman who flaunted herself, and gave herself to many men, and who would not obey nor pay homage to the Sabbath. What they said of me made no difference—I was haughty and self-absorbed, a woman lost in the world—and not even knowing she was lost. Worse, I was lost from my real Self—the Self that the Master spoke of, the Self that is forever . . .

I . . . I . . . Forgive me . . . I cannot hold the quill in stillness to write properly, and the precious ink that is brought to me daily by a kind stranger is splattering upon the parchment. I can hear the screaming in the streets above me as the ignorant ones from the darkness hunt down the Master's followers. They are killing anyone who was ever seen with Jesus. They strike down and kill anyone who speaks his name. I try to forgive them even as my friends' blood runs in the streets . . . and it is hard . . . so hard. For I am human—and my human self wants to lash out at these beasts who, in their ignorance, lash out and kill those who desire to worship God in Spirit, those who are persecuting us. But I can hear the words of the Master, the words he spoke with his dying breath, "Forgive them, O Father, for they know not what they do . . . " God grant me the ability do likewise. God give me the strength to do so. Forgive me, Master. The ink runs blurry across the page with my tears . . . I think of my friends who I cannot help, who are screaming, who are dying. I must stop for now, for ink and tears will make this unreadable . . . Master . . . help them . . . help me . . . I cannot write hearing their voices . . . *please help them . . .*

It is now dawn and all is quiet. A gentle soul has come down and left me bread and water. Refilled my alabaster jar that holds the precious ink and has provided me more parchment. He removes the pages that I have written the night before. One of the Master's closest followers, his Disciple, Andrew, assured me before he took flight to other lands that my writings would be kept in a secret hiding place. Before he left, he kissed my hand and said, "Write it all, Mary, all that you remember. For we must be about the Master's ministry and his teachings of love Divine, and tell as many people who will listen. Someone will come for you in the weeks to come and take you to safety. Until that time, write it all. Godspeed, Mary, keep the faith."

Since that time, this gentle stranger brings me food and drink and gathers my writings before the dawn's first light, leaves me with enough food for the day and then disappears into the dangers of the streets above. I do not even know his name, but I know he risks his very life to give me these precious things.

So I must find the words of all the things He did and said, and pray that one day it will find the light of day. Trust and faith are all I have . . . now—and his promise. For these I am grateful.

I can look back through the darkened hallways of my memories and the day of my Beginning—the beginning of the death of my old self, and the birth of my new self—stands out as no other. As I said in the beginning, it was a day of death and a day of birth. For I was a woman of the world before the Master came. I say that with no shame, none at all. I was one who had many lovers, and I gave myself freely to many men. I was searching for love. Not knowing then that the love I sought was something far more powerful than love of the body.

One morning I awoke and I heard a pounding upon the door. There was shouting and suddenly the door gave way. The man with whom I lay shoved me upon the dirty floor, as if I were a plague. Then I saw the priests, the members of the Sanhedrin standing in the doorway before me. After being knocked to the floor, I was dragged from that room by my hair. I managed to pull a linen blanket around me to cover my nakedness. I hit my head on the ornate bedpost, and then upon the stone floor . . . then all I remember was pain and bewilderment. My bewilderment didn't last long. While two of the men dragged and whipped me, another was speaking, reading off a litany of charges, crimes that I had supposedly committed. I remember being slapped and kicked and then thrown down the stone steps leading to the streets. The flesh of my back and my legs and arms was torn, shredded—but I felt no pain. I was numb. Blood can flow, my friends, long before pain is felt, and that was my experience. I held on tight to the linen sheet that covered me. I was surprised to see that he who dragged me through the streets was a man not unknown to me. He had visited me, this member of the religious order of the day—more than once. Once my lover, now he was my persecutor. I had loved him once, now I was betrayed—how I loathed him! I tried in vain to fight, but by the time we reached the streets he had the assistance of other church henchmen, thirsty for sacrifice. They spit upon me and called me harlot. They kicked me even while I was dragged over the rock-strewn street. As if I weren't bloody enough, they lashed my legs and back and breasts with leather straps.

Mind you, I am not the same person now as I was then. Then . . . well . . . then I was a called a woman cursed of seven devils. I was hated. I was envied. I was called a mystery, an abomination, and I did not care. I was a woman divorced from my own soul. Above all, I was scorned, for I did not hold to religious rituals for a ritual's sake. I paid no heed to the high priests' observances of holy days. I didn't know the Sabbath from any other day. On this day, *that* was my downfall. For I was caught, on a Holy Day, performing unholy acts, with a Roman, and I was going to pay for it with my blood, my life.

My sentence for such a crime, little did I know, was death. Though I was only twenty-three at the time, I felt a yearning for death. For I found no solace, no peace, no comfort in any place with any man, any luxury, any thing. I was like a stranger to the earth, often bewildered to find myself walking upon it. I was a walking dead woman then. But here, now, I regret not one thing. Had I not walked the streets and befriended the night, I never would have known the beauty of the dawn, and the light. The Master represented the dawn, the Light, and He saved me from the eternal night of fruitless yearning and desires unfulfilled. Yes, for all that I experienced, I am grateful.

But then . . . well . . . they hurtled me into a pit of stones, a place of shame and scorn and, yes, death. The blood from other dead criminals was crusted and dried upon the rocks upon which I landed. In these times, amid the tyranny of the Roman rule, it takes very little to find one's self brought up on charges—or to be in the place where I was: in the pit of execution. For between the Romans and the hypocrites who were in charge of the law and the churches, few of us—people like me— had a chance. I was not a woman of prayer in those days but as I lay among the rocks I did pray.

Let it be quick, I prayed, pleaded. *Please let it end quickly.* The reading of my crimes went on and on—the charges that were being read. Some of the charges were true, most were not. I was called harlot, committing blasphemy, by consorting with a Roman soldier on a Holy Sabbath day. I heard the Sanhedrin priest, but I did not listen—I wrapped what was left of the bloody linen around my body and rested my head upon the stones.

Just end it, I thought. *Throw your stones and end my miserable life.* But, it was not quick. The priest droned on and on, and people were shouting at me—the most despicable, terrible things. It was when he finished reading the trumped-up charges and I knew death was near, that I heard another voice—a voice that commanded *everyone's* attention.

It was a man's voice but I had never heard anyone speak with such clarity, such strength, such authority.

For a strange moment I thought, *is that the voice of God?* Little did I know, but that thought was closer to the truth than I would ever know. I uncovered my eyes and looked in the direction of the voice, but I couldn't see the man. The sunlight was behind him and I was blinded by the light.

"Who are *you* to condemn this woman?" the Voice asked.

"I speak with the authority of Moses' law!" said the priest. "This . . . this . . . *woman* was caught in an unspeakable act on the Sabbath. According to Moses' law, her punishment is death by stoning."

I didn't move much, lying in that dreadful place, but I kept trying to see who had the courage to speak up for me—*me*—of all people. All I saw was a light, and powerful male form, tall and well-built, with a booming voice. As the priest answered, I couldn't believe it but I think I actually heard this man, who had come to my defense, laugh.

"And you've never sinned?" the stranger asked the priest. "This woman is no stranger to *you*, is she? Why, you have visited her . . . let's see . . . how many times has it been—at least . . . six maybe seven times." He chuckled again at the priest who was obviously shaken. For it was true—how did this man know that I had been with this priest? So many questions ran through my mind, for a moment I had forgotten my own impending death.

"*Silence!*" the priest shouted. "I have never consorted with this woman on a Holy Day!"

"Everyday is a holy day," the Voice said. "The Sabbath was made for man, not the other way around." Uneasy whisperings, gasps, and murmuring were heard around the stone pit. By now I could see the man. He was extraordinarily handsome. He seemed to tower over the priest and did so without fear. His hair almost red, close-cropped beard, deep, penetrating eyes—like the blue-gray of storm clouds. Quite honestly, he was the most beautiful man I had ever seen.

"Who are you?" the priest asked. "And who do you represent?"

"I too am a priest, but of a different order," the man said. "I have come to have you—all of you—consider the truth in a new light. To consider the *spirit* of the law *and not the letter of the law.* Are any of you without sin upon your soul? Who among you has never sinned?" His voice boomed like thunder. "If you are without sin, cast your stone!"

I covered my head—but no rock was thrown. The crowd only murmured uneasily. But mostly there was silence. No one moved. Some people shuffled restlessly and looked at the ground.

As grateful as I was for someone to stand up for me, I believed I would not be dying alone in this dreadful pit of stones, but I would have company—the company of the man who was speaking so recklessly on my behalf. I watched as the man knelt upon the ground and invited the crowd—(especially those with rocks in their hands, ready to end my life) to look at something he was writing or drawing in the dust of the road. Moving very slowly, I removed the bloody linen from my face, and looked upon the crowd and this unusual man.

I watched as people walked behind this man and read what he was writing. Without exception all of them gasped and covered their faces and turned away—some running away. *What could he be writing in the dust to make people drop their rocks and forget their thirst for my blood?* Whatever it was, it was horrifying to the crowd and I—the condemned—was forgotten at least for the moment. My execution, for the moment, was stayed. Some of the crowd stumbled backwards, dropping their stones, looking at this strange, beautiful man, who never ceased to smile as he wrote in the dirt, their faces ashen with shock. I didn't know what they were running from—but I didn't care. I was happy they were leaving—and dropping their stones. Suddenly, I realized I didn't want to die. Not here. Not like this.

With the sun shining brightly in the eastern sky, I could see the expressions clearly upon the faces of those gathered around the man as he wrote on and on. I will never forget the smile upon this man's face as he wrote. When he would pause, he would look to a person in the crowd, and write again. As if by some unknown magic, a miracle occurred. One by one they went away. As I said, many *ran* away. From my viewpoint, I was surprised to see even the most blood-thirsty members of the mob looking at me with complete disgust, and yet when they gazed down upon ground at what the man had written, some gasped, some screamed and *every one of them ran away*! They dropped their stones— some cast them away from them as if they contained a deadly poison.

All the while the man continued to write on and on.

Mind you, I was only a moment away from my death before this man arrived. Now, suddenly I was alone with no persecutors in sight— except for one. The priest who read my crimes was still standing, far apart from this man. He would not walk over to where this man was kneeling beside the execution pit. The priest looked like a man who suddenly found himself lost in a foreign country. Upon his face were expressions of anger, confusion, bewilderment. After watching this strange spectacle of people "reading and running", the priest finally stormed over to the man who was writing. This man, who I would soon come to know as Jesus, finished his writing and stood up as the priest approached.

"Read it," the Master said, pointing to the ground. His words were a command.

The priest looked at Jesus and attempted to speak to the Master and again, that booming voice sounded: *"Read what I have written!"*

For the first time, I saw that the priest was frightened. Then he looked at the ground. It must have been the sun shining in my eyes—but it seemed to me that the priest began to shrink in stature. His face became a mask of shame—a grimace of shame, remorse, regret. He lowered his head, uttered a strangled sob, covered his face and ran away, just as the others had done. He did not lift his eyes again before he fled.

I was bewildered—and confused. I had no idea what had happened except my life had been spared. What did the priest see written in the sand? What did those people read, those who sought to stone me to death? I later learned they saw their own sin. In some way that to this day I'll never understand, in whatever the Master wrote in the sand, each saw the secret sin they would never tell anyone. I do not know how it was that each person saw their own shame written in the dust. I don't know the *how* the Master did many things that he did. But I knew one thing—he had saved my life. I laid my head upon the rocks and wept.

In the midst of the stones and blood and sand and my tears, he walked down into the stoning pit and knelt beside me. He gently lifted my hand and kissed it. I looked into his eyes and for the first time in my life I felt loved. I didn't know him, but yet I felt that I did somehow, in

some other time, or in a dream perhaps. He was a familiar stranger—
and I felt loved like I had never been loved before. I knew as I gazed
into his eyes that he knew everything I had ever done, ever said, ever
thought. Sounds incredible, I know, but I knew it in my heart. And
unlike anyone else I had ever known, I knew he did not judge me.

"Where are your persecutors, my lady?" He asked, a smile playing
across his lips.

Tears of gratitude and astonishment poured down my cheeks. "There
are none, sir." My emotions choked off any further words and I wrapped
my arms around his neck. "Thank you," I whispered. It was all I could
say.

"Lady Mary Magdalene," He said, cradling my head in his large hands.
"You can get up now. Let me help you." His voice was like the call of
spring after a long, hard winter. He picked me up and it was like everything was new when I was in his arms—a feeling of homecoming—and
I felt like a bride. He kissed my forehead and carried me out of the pit.
I was astonished, for I could feel the bruises and bloodied cuts on my
body disappearing. I felt bathed in a warm light—a light that took away
all pain, stopped the draining blood from my body. He wrapped the
linen around me carefully, covering my nakedness.

As the Master carried me I found my voice and said, "You . . . you do
not condemn me?" He smiled and it was like the heavy weight of the
world was lifted from me.

"Neither do I condemn you, Mary. We have much to do. You are
loved more than you know." At the sound of his voice, I cried, leaning
my head once more upon his chest, wrapping my arms around his
neck.

As he carried me, there was healing not only of my bruised body but
of my mind and spirit. I felt . . . *renewed* . . . *born again*. I'd never felt such
power, such . . . *love* . . . in all my life. As he set me down, I found myself
standing before a group of men. Again, there was a feeling as if I'd come
home. In that moment, it was like everything that was dead in me became alive. I *knew* that this man saw and understood every crime, every
sinful deed I'd ever done—and yet—what shone through his eyes was a
love indescribable. I knew he loved every unlovable thing about me.

Tears streamed down my face and I was ashamed—but he saw not the scarlet of my sins, only the light of my soul. For the first time, I could feel that I was more than just a physical being—I felt myself to be so much more . . . it is hard to explain. It was as if my entire life up to that point had led to this moment. It felt like I had found my destiny and yet, I did not know what that meant. There was something different about him, the Master, from other men, and this was the feeling from the group who followed him. They would eventually become my closest friends and allies. And they welcomed me into their circle.

As the Master set me down in front of his friends, the garment that was just a bloody sheet moments before was now a beautiful toga-like dress. There was no blood on my hands, legs, or face. My hair had untangled and I wondered if I had found myself in a wonderful dream.

The Master then turned to his band of friends who would soon become my friends and he said, "My friends, this is Mary—the Magdalene—and she will be with us wherever we go."

He looked into my eyes and there—in that moment—I knew I was home. Who he was, I knew not, but I knew I never wanted to be away from him for a single moment—for the rest of my life. He saved me, and this was a time when I myself did not consider myself worth saving. As I said, it was the day of my death, and it was the day of my rebirth. My life would never again be the same.

Before the Master came into my life, I had made my home in Jerusalem, away from my parents. I had left home at an early age under tragic circumstances. As I said, I always felt like I was a stranger to the earth. I was so different from my older sister Martha, and older brother Lazarus. They were so different from me and had moved out of the family household before I left it. My father ruled the household and was strict. Because I yearned to be part of the world, I was not, in my father's eyes, behaving the way a young girl of fifteen should be. I rebelled against the religious observances. I argued with my father of the ways in which women were treated (my mother always walked several paces behind my father when they were out in public—such is the custom still—but was never the custom with the Master. With him, I walked side by side.) And so my early life was turbulent—and as I grew older the turbulence grew greater. I wanted to dress in finery, and be a part of the world—the world where people danced and drank wine and celebrated life. This was not the way of my family life. And the day came when I had no choice but to leave the home of my parents and search for the "something" my restless soul longed for.

My mother was always critical of me—especially when I would paint my eyes or my lips and go out in the evening with my friends. She never hid her disdain or the disapproval. I would often sneak out the back door of our cottage, and meet with other girls. In my heart I think she was jealous of me. For I didn't look like the other girls my age. I looked like a woman. And felt like a woman, but not a woman of my mother's era. A drudge, a scrubwoman, a char, a thing. A thing that could cook and clean and be used and sometimes abused at the whim of the man she married, my father. I was ashamed to watch her walking behind my father when they went to Temple. I felt an indescribable anger as I watched all the women walk behind their husbands when out in public. Not allowed to walk side by side, even though they shared the same bed in the same house. They slept side by side, why can't they walk side by side in public. I once (and only once) asked my mother and my father this question.

"It's not right," I said to my parents, ignoring the shocked expressions on both of their faces. "A man and his wife sit at the same table, break bread together, have children together and yet, in public, she is not worthy to walk side by side. What is the matter with the world?"

My father leaped at me like a cat. He slapped the left side of my face, and then the right. I fell to the floor.

"Who do you think you are?" my father screamed at me, his whole body shaking with rage, his furrowed face bright red. I had, with my question, unleashed the beast that often came out unprovoked against my mother. Now, as I was approaching womanhood, my father struck me down in the same manner as he had with my mother. As I lay there, I knew I was a woman now. My father believed women were to be put in their place and that was a place of silence. This is why so often I felt I had been born as a stranger to the earth, for I felt myself equal to all people—men and women. And so, when I met the Master, he treated all in the same manner. He showed forth unconditional love to all people and treated all equally.

When my father would be abusive to my mother, what confounded me was her lack of anger, the lack of retaliation—even within her own self, I could see she came to believe that my father was right, and she was wrong—especially on the rare occasion she gave her opinion on some subject. That was what would enrage my father the most. Horses were treated better than the wives, the women of my day. So I grew up angry, and I cultivated my anger, like a nightshade garden. I vowed in my heart that the day would come when I would not only walk side by side but hand in hand with a man. Let the old traditions be damned. The only women that walked side by side with a man in those days were the women of the night, the outcasts who wore fine clothes and drank fine wine and were not betrothed to any man. I would see them in Jerusalem and was warned by my parents against even looking at them—for they were called *creatures* by my mother and father. And yet, I watched my father look at one of these "creatures" one day as we went to Jerusalem on a buying trip. He was a man both vexed and hypnotized. I saw in his eyes . . . longing and disapproval . . . and, although he would never admit this, *admiration* of the woman's beauty.

I stood for a long while and I watched a woman with golden hair, not covered by a veil, but flowing over her bare shoulders in golden ringlets. She was like a beautiful statue from the Grecian Isles. She wore gold and silver and a long dress obviously made in Persia. She had painted lips and her eyelids were shaded in dark hues of brown and silver, painted to the eyebrows. To me she looked like a goddess. And the men that surrounded her! She was attended to by handsome men—and walked arm-in-arm with a man of obvious wealth. To me she looked like a queen. People of the streets walked by her and scowled—some called her names of ill repute. Rather than anger, she responded to them with laughter. I can still hear the obscenities she shouted back at them—all the while laughing, being held and kissed—*in public*. I thought no one would ever dream of slapping that woman to the ground. I could tell by the men surrounding her that she was protected. And woe to the unfortunate individual (a man not unlike my father) who would dare to touch her when she did not desire to be touched! Such a man, I knew in my heart, would be knocked to the ground, just as I was by my own father.

I kept all these things secret in my heart—but I knew my destiny when I saw the golden-haired women in the streets of Jerusalem. I would be no one's slave. No one's whipping post. That was death to me. You see I had no choice, really. And I chose life. My day of decision had arrived when my father slapped me to the floor while my mother stood by and watched. There would be no saving grace in this house. No rescue. I could look forward, if I followed my father's wishes, to an arranged marriage with another man like my father, no doubt . . . love meant nothing, and was not required. What was required was a house and children and walking eight paces behind the man I would be betrothed to. And beatings.

Is it any wonder, my friends, that I chose the life that I did? Better to be an outcast and live than follow strict, narrow-minded, hard-hearted tradition and be the walking dead—as so many of the women were, my mother included. No. I would not.

It is quite peculiar and amazing how all of this flashed through my mind as I lay upon the floor, still feeling the stinging slap of my father's hand on my face. I remember seeing the blood running from my bruised lips, dropping upon stone floor. As I lifted myself to a half-sitting position, ignoring the blood that ran down my chin, I smiled at my father.

He stepped back from me, the smile clearly confounded and confused him. That made me smile all the more.

"Mary," my mother pleaded, "You know better than to ask . . . questions . . . of the law . . . and to question your father . . . you . . . you—"

I turned my gaze to my mother, my smile never wavering. She faltered because I wiped the blood from my mouth onto my hand. I held it out, like an indictment, against my father—and my mother. They did not care I was hurt. They did not care I was bleeding. They only cared that I was not in my "proper place."

My father's defiance and anger seemed to melt when he looked at the blood on my face, my hand.

"Mary," he started to say, his voice wavering between confusion and anger.

"No," I said. "You would strike me down for asking a question. My, it is a good thing, is it not, that I haven't committed some crime. What would you have done to me then, Father? Killed me, no doubt."

"Mary!" My mother exclaimed—it was a frightened plea, the whimpering of a martyr. I was disgusted with her, and wounded that she would not come to my defense

"Mary," my father began, trying to control his voice. How odd, my father had no control. I knew then I had him right where I wanted him.

"No," I said again. "You are not talking now. *I am*. And you will listen—both of you. And so help me, Father, if you raise a hand to me again, you better raise it for the last time, and finish me off for good. If you do not, then I will invoke the gods of wrath and I will murder you in your sleep and burn down this house."

Gasps from my parents. I slowly stood up, and faced them both. I knew this was the last day I would ever call this place my home. And I was glad.

At the same time, tears mingled with the blood on my face and my voice threatened to falter, but I would not let it. My father seemed to fall into his chair rather than sit in it. He looked at me like I was a dangerous, wild animal—he thought it best to retreat. That was wise. I was, in that moment, dangerous—out of my own mind with rage and hurt. Not because he had struck me down and physically hurt me—but that he had no respect, no love, for me, his daughter. I could even endure the knowing he didn't love me, but to not see me as a human being but only as a *thing*, like he viewed my own mother—that was the breaking point. This is where the first of the many devils possessed me. I was filled with malicious anger, the desire for vengeance—the desire for this violent, domineering, evil-minded man to die a slow painful death. It was the beginning of a possession of numerous dark spirits that would take hold of me in the years to come. Until *He*, the Master came. In that moment I was an instrument of wrath. I stood up to the monster of a man who was my father.

My mother dissolved into convulsive sobbing after I hurled the epithets at my father. She backed away from me and my father, horror etched upon her face. She ran from the room as if she had found herself in a cage of man-eating lions. I tried to understand her fleeing, but in my heart I knew that if I and my mother would have been in a lion's den, she would have run to save herself alone, forgetting her daughter, leaving her to be ripped to shreds.

But in this den, no one would be ripped to shreds—except in the heart. And the final words I said to my father came forth from the dark demons of wrath, fury, and indignation. Again, let me remind you this was *before the Master came.* I say this not as an excuse but just as a fact. I had been under siege in this household by a tyrant of a father, who, as I said, would take the leather strap to my mother if the evening meal was late, if he suspected she was gone from the house too long, if she ever disagreed with him. Oh, and when he drank too much wine or other spirits, these brought out the worst in him and he was known for brawling in the streets, and then . . . well, then the devil would come home—and my mother . . . she received the remaining violent rage. I had heard that my sister and brother would huddle hidden in the upstairs closet and weep . . . they were afraid, not for themselves but afraid he was going to kill her.

The memories of those times further fueled the venomous rage I felt toward my father. I'll never forget his face after he fell into his chair, in a state of shock. He looked like a man who was going insane—as if some inanimate object—a table, or chair, had begun to speak aloud to him. The way he understood women, that they were objects, things, I can see now why he was so astonished. For in his mind, his wife, his daughters were nothing but tables and chairs. And tables and chairs do not speak. Neither did my mother for all those years. So I spoke for her—and for me.

Remembering how he leapt at me, like a cat, before he struck me, before I finished the final words I would ever say to him, I picked up the ornamental dagger that hung upon the wall and unsheathed it. *Only if he leaps at me again,* I thought, *this is my protection.* In the darker recesses of my mind, part of me wished that he *would* leap at me again. I would have gladly destroyed him—this monster—and freed my mother from her slavery. But that's not the way things happened, thank goodness. It is easy to see, is it not, that I was a person possessed by many demons?

My father's eyes widened as he saw me slowly retrieve the dagger from the wall. My father collected relics, weapons, from all over the world. He displayed them on the wall. I carefully pulled the dagger free from the leather sheath, never taking my eyes from my father. I glanced down at the knife and saw the intricate and detailed ivory handle, and the gleaming silver of the blade . . . though old, it was razor sharp even still. It felt *good* in my hand. I would not use it. Not unless I had to.

My father looked at me like a stranger—a dangerous, irrational stranger.

"I know you are waiting to raise your voice and order me from the house," I said. "Say not a word to me, Father, I warn you. I *am* leaving your house. There is to be no more shouting, no more violence. Not to me, and not to that frightened creature in the kitchen. I despise what you have done to her, to me, to all of us. You've turned my mother into a frightened, tortured *thing*. May the gods be merciful to your soul, but because you have shown no mercy, no love, no care—rest assured that you will die a bitter, angry old man. As the years pass you've grown more bitter, more angry, and no one—*no one*—in this household knows why. Mother has done everything for you. You've provided us with a material life of physical comforts more than most families will ever enjoy. But oh, the price we've all had to pay—especially Mother. Know this, and heed this well, Father. *I will be watching out for Mother.* She will not know where I am going, neither will you, so don't you dare try to beat it out of her. *She . . . will . . . not . . . know where I am.*

"But I will check up on Mother. Do not worry, you will never see me again. But I will be seeing you. If you ever again hurt her, I will find you. And finish you."

To my surprise, my father lowered his head and wept. I can still see him running his hands through his hair, curling them into fists and . . . it seemed like he was going to tear his hair out. He shook his head slowly back and forth, tears falling upon the alabaster floor, the Persian rug. I felt . . . nothing at all. My mother quietly came out of the kitchen, but stood out of sight.

"It's all right, Mother," I said, not turning to meet her gaze. "Father will never again strike you, or hurt you. As I said while you were with the servants in the kitchen, if he ever lifts a hand to you, I will find out—and he will be hunted down and then know how it feels to be on the receiving end of irrational rage and violence."

"Mary, please," Mother said. "Don't leave like this . . . not like this. He didn't mean to hurt you . . . he just . . . loses his temper and isn't himself when he—when he—"

"When he whips you until your back bleeds because you forgot to bake bread for dinner, Mother?" I asked.

She once again wept and started to leave the room. I grabbed her arm.

"It's over, Mother. He'll never do it again, unless he wants to die."

"Mary, this isn't you talking," Mother said. "Your father has provided for us, you've never wanted for anything—look at this beautiful home!"

"Mother," I said. "I've wanted and been starved for the most important thing a daughter could ever want."

"I gave you everything!" my father said, his voice breaking with tears.

"No, you didn't," I said. "You forgot the most important thing of all. Love. You never loved me."

I turned to my mother, and embraced her. "I love you."

"Mary," my father said, gazing at me with haunted eyes, "I didn't mean . . . I never meant to . . . to . . . " His words trailed off. I embraced my mother and started upstairs to my room to gather my things and pack. Half way up the stairs, I looked down at my father. "It's over," I said. "I am going."

"Where?" Mother asked. "Where will you go, Mary? You can't just—go to the streets! A woman alone? In these times? Why—"

"I can't tell you, Mother. But I'll write and I promise you, I'll *watch for you*—in case . . . " My father looked up at me, his anger gone, tears filling his eyes. "Well, just in case . . . something should happen. Then, I'll send for you," I said.

After that, I left for Jerusalem—and I sought to find the golden-haired woman I had seen months before. And I found her. Her name was Marcella and she too was considered an "outcast." She had a beautiful home in a picturesque area of Jerusalem. It was because of Marcella that I became educated in so many ways. She took me under her wing—and welcomed me like a daughter. I found the terrible things that were whispered about her were untrue—she was one of the kindest people I would ever meet. But she, like me, was also a stranger to the earth, and of society. And she taught me not to care what people think about you. She introduced me to people of nobility, of many walks of life. There have been many things said of me, but it was because of Marcella that

I was never affected by the disapproving glances of the masses that followed tradition for tradition's sake.

Yes, it is true, I met many men and had many lovers. And I did not know it at the time, but when I met Him, the Master, I realized that all the time I was searching for love in so many places, I was searching for Him.

On that day I was saved from the pit—I knew that yet another chapter of my life was over, was ended, and a new chapter was beginning.

Meeting the Master was the dawning of that new chapter—and I had no idea the heights that I would experience with Him. It was because of the Master that I was reunited with my family. Not my father—no, he had passed on some four years after I had left home. But my mother, Martha, and Lazarus—we would be together again—and it was because of the Master that that miracle occurred.

The hour grows late and the oil lamp grows dim. I must stop at this point and rest. There is still so much to tell. And, now—I feel the Master's beloved presence with me, whispering to me, "Goodnight, Mary."

2

When Lazarus Died—
and Lived Again

Imagine for a moment what God would look like if he came to earth as a man. Imagine the contours of his face— deep blue eyes that when you gazed into them, you felt like you were floating in a warm ocean—held by the waves, a gentle rhythm. This is what happened to those who gazed into Jesus' eyes. You could feel God right there. I write this boldly and almost broke my quill—because I desire so much to describe the indescribable beauty of this man whose eyes were windows to the heavenly worlds beyond our sight or imaginings. But you could indeed glimpse those worlds in the Master's eyes, and when he spoke it was like a great singing wind—all the elements of the earth and sky con- verged and spoke aloud in his voice. It was music—crystal and clear—and deep. When he spoke of the Unseen Father- Mother-God he would almost whisper, and yet every one around him could hear—even those who were seated far away from him. Their soul heard the Voice of its Maker. That is what I mean. When he spoke, he awakened the sleeping souls from their self-absorbed selves.

Jesus, the man, was the love of God made manifest. When he spoke, the Universe spoke. When he walked upon the earth and passed by a house, those who dwelled therein felt a stirring, a yearning beyond their understanding. I know this because my own sister, Martha, experienced the Master in this way. Before she first met him, she had heard stories of a man who performed miraculous healings and was a prophet, and there were whisperings that he was the Messiah.

My sister Martha and I were as different as night and day. When I left the family, I did not seek her out, nor did I seek out my brother Lazarus. I did not know it, but long before the Master saved me from death, my sister and Lazarus were acquainted and friends with the Master. After we were reunited, Martha told me of the day that she first saw the Master. It was an extraordinary experience. As usual, my sister was always busy around the house. She was always cleaning when it was sparkling already. She could never sit still. And she told me one day while she swept out the cobwebs from my brother Lazarus' bedroom, she said she felt a wave of complete and total love fill the room, and fill her heart. It was as if there was a great flood of water that swept through the house, and swept through my sister.

"It was like hearing the voice of an angel say 'I love you, Martha!' I know how silly that sounds," she said, "but that's what it was like. I dropped the broom and felt like my feet didn't touch the floor. I found myself outside. And there . . . he was. Walking down the road. I felt him before I ever saw him. And then he turned his wondrous face toward me and smiled." Martha, my ever-placid sister who rarely showed any emotion (except an urgency to clean) wept, when she told me this. Like a child she said, "I've never seen anyone like that man before. I knew he loved me and he didn't even know me! It was strange but not strange. It was like I had forgotten a very intimate and beautiful dream and then when I looked into his eyes, I remembered. I remembered that I was loved by that being—the one he calls the Father-Mother-God of All That Is. I knew I was loved—and I knew I was a *part* of that great being.

And I ran to him like a silly schoolgirl! And he opened wide his arms and I . . . " her voice—even today when she tells this story, breaks with emotion and tears, "I knew I was home." That is what she said. "I was home."

Being with Jesus was always like a homecoming. Imagine for a moment that you forgot where you lived. Now imagine that you forgot all of the people who lived in the house—your family—who loved you. You have no memory of the days, the hours, the years you lived and loved in that house. Then, imagine looking into the eyes of the most beautiful creature you can bring to mind, and then remembering. Remembering your home, your family, and above all else that you are cherished and loved beyond any description by these people in the home. That's what it was like when I sat with Jesus and listened to him and talked with him. He brought back to my little mind, that I had a greater mind—an eternal one—one that would never, ever die—but would live on beyond after death. Just being in the presence of the Master, Jesus, made most people feel this way. Not all. No. He had enemies. There were times when we were afraid someone would try to kill him. But if the crowds who came to him for healing became too unruly, he would simply vanish. We would find him later walking in the Palestine hills. So often, the Master would reassure us that all was well. We did not know then that he was going to eventually be facing the ultimate challenge, the hardest test. I will write more of that when I have the strength.

For now, I wish to rest in the most profound love I've ever known—sitting in His shadow by that olive tree near my old house. In the quiet, there was divine quiet. It was like the silence rang—rang with complete harmony—like a secret symphony that is only played and heard in the heart. The music of the soul is the silence. I do not mean the absence of sound, no. This is the Silence—where God can come into the heart and mind and sit for a while, just . . . loving you . . . and you know that you are that Creator's child . . . and you always will be . . . forever . . . and that there will be world and universes without end to be lived and loved in . . . always and forever—the dance of the soul with its Maker. It is a dance. It is a romance—God is romance and intimacy and all things lovely. The Master taught us: "When you feel completely at peace with yourself and your lover, your partner—imagine that magnified a hundred-fold and then you will have some idea of what the Unseen God feels for Its creations—you—the souls, the sons and daughters of God in the earth."

And so it was I went with the Master to the home of my sister and brother Lazarus. My mother had come to live with them after my father's death.

I crossed the threshold of my sister's home, the Master by my side.

"Miriam," the Master said to my mother, "Your daughter has come home."

My mother turned with a start, her eyes filled with tears. I wept as I felt her arms around me, she too was gently sobbing.

"Behold," my mother said, "My daughter who was dead has come back to life." I knew then that she too had been touched by the Master's words in some way or manner. Through blurring tears I looked and I saw my sister, Martha. In younger years, she had been harsh and judgmental with me. I could see that she too was changed and she came and embraced me. We were a family again, and there was the feeling of homecoming.

"The house that was once divided is now whole again," the Master said. "May the blessings of God shine down upon all of you."

After the Master had spoken those words, he placed hands upon each of us in turn and blessed us. In that moment, we were filled with the light of love too indescribable for words. We felt like children again. Even through tears there was laughter and joy—and we danced together in a circle. The Master laughed and truly it is one of the finest memories of my life.

My mother turned to the Master. "Thank you," she said, "for bringing my daughter home to us." The Master bowed to her and then again said a blessing upon us. Before he could reach the door, Martha again put her arms around the Master's neck and embraced him.

"I will be making a celebratory meal tomorrow," Martha said. "Can you come and join us? Please bring all of your friends."

"It would be an honor, dear Martha." And quietly he left with his Disciples, who were waiting outside the door.

"Where is Lazarus?" I asked. I was so anxious to see my brother and wondered why he wasn't present.

"Lazarus went into town some hours ago," Martha said. "He's late, as usual. I'm sure he will be home directly."

My newly reunited family watched from the front door as the Master went his way. There were throngs of people who had gathered in front of our house when word spread that the Master was there. My sister's home was near the seashore and we watched as he boarded the boat with his Disciples. The multitudes clamored to follow the boat, but John pushed off shore, and we watched until the ship was just a small dot in the distance.

It was amazing to see so many people following this man. And what was further amazing is that before he boarded the boat, many of the people who came were limp, sick, or lame. The Master would go to the children first. He would lay his hand upon their head, look up to the sky and then smile into the eyes of the child. I thought I heard the Master say to the children, "You are like the kingdom of God—sweet and innocent and loving. Go forward, now, you are healed." He had a special way with the children, and they loved him. More than once, I saw him whisper something into their ears and behold—I saw the miraculous, right in front of my own home. Those with withered limbs suddenly were made whole. People who were laying upon stretchers got up after the Master touched and blessed them. As he made his way through the crowd, every one that the Master touched was healed. As there had been sounds of celebration in my own house, there were celebrations in the streets as well. Children who could not walk, were running, skipping, dancing behind the Master.

"He *is* the Chosen One," my mother said, dabbing tears from her eyes. "He is the One we have looked to come to us, for so long—the Messiah."

At that time, I was only twenty-three years old, and was not educated in the ways of the ancient prophets. In my heart, I knew that I was in the presence of an extraordinary being, when I was with the Master, Jesus. I vowed that I would read all the sacred writings, speak with the Master whenever I could.

"Mother, I am going to follow him," I said.

"Child, it is your destiny, I believe," she said. We hugged again and there was so much I wanted to ask her, so much I wanted to say. I felt remorse at the way I had left my home—I felt ashamed. But as soon as those feelings surfaced, it was as if I could feel the Master's touch upon me, and those feelings were replaced with something else. For the first time, I think I was beginning to feel my Spirit—my own soul—that I had been out of touch with for so long—so long.

At that moment there was a noise in the back of the house—the sound of a door opening and someone was coughing—a harsh and deep cough—and then there was a thump upon the floor. I thought that perhaps it was one of the members of the crowd who had come to the Master for healing. We hurried to the back door and it was my brother Lazarus. The contents of the bags he had carried from town were strewn all over the floor. He was barely aware of us, his eyes were glazed and his body was shaking all over.

"Lazarus!" My mother exclaimed. She placed a hand upon his forehead. "Mary, quickly, help me get him to his room." When I looked upon his face, I felt a coldness in the pit of my stomach. *Oh please, God, not the Fever. Let him not have the Fever.* A raging sickness had been running through many parts of Jerusalem—and the people who contracted it rarely got well—the outcome was . . . at the time I couldn't fathom the idea that I might lose the brother I had just been reunited with.

Mother, Martha and I carried Lazarus to his bedchamber. He was delirious with fever. I quickly soaked some wool towels in cold water, outside from the rain barrel. Lazarus thrashed upon the bed, his eyes were yellow-tinted—and he didn't seem to recognize us. We undressed him and covered him in cold cloths, attempting to stay the fever. Martha immediately sent to the city for a physician and I dispatched one of her servants to Bethabra—a small town not far from my sister's home in Bethsaida, where Martha said the Master might be staying—to tell him that Lazarus was ill.

Lazarus had all the symptoms I had seen before in this illness. His eyes had a yellowish cast and the sweat ran off of him in buckets. I don't believe he ever regained consciousness during the illness. The physician came and examined him and shook his head.

"I am sorry, Miriam," the physician said to my mother, "but he has the Fever." My mother wept and nearly fainted. We led her to the chair.

"I am leaving a tincture that will enable him to sleep with more ease, and will ease any pain he may have. Place several drops of this under his tongue every few hours. It is not a cure, but it will keep him comfortable."

"Is there . . . is there nothing we can do?" my mother asked, tears choking her voice.

"I am sorry," the physician said. "But protect yourselves as much as you can—cover your faces when you are near his bedside—for this fever is a contagion."

My mother, sister, and I held out hope that the servant would be able to find the Master—for we knew that he could make Lazarus well again. We took turns staying with Lazarus—giving him the tincture and praying by his bed. My mother was inconsolable. This was her firstborn.

"If only he had come in just a few minutes before the Master," she wailed. "If only . . . "

"Don't, mother," Martha said. "There is still time for the Master to come." But time was running short. His fever was raging and he had slipped into a deep sleep—the sleep of the dying.

When mother was able to speak, she would reminisce about Lazarus—and I was amazed when she said that Jesus and he were childhood friends. Lazarus was some ten years older than I—and I had no idea my mother was acquainted with Him.

"This man, Jesus, was a special child," my mother said. "It seemed to me that he was always beyond us in some way. I had heard rumors, at the time I didn't believe, but now . . . now I believe the stories were true."

"What were they, Mother?"

"It was said that if someone were sick, they could merely touch his garment and they were healed. Some people called him 'a lucky charm.' Now I know it was true." She looked off to the sky. "And that he has come to this house, and blessed us—is more than I could ever have dreamed of. She smiled through the tears. Now if only he would come . . . if only . . . "

Her voice trailed off . . . I wanted so much to apologize to her for the way I had left, but I couldn't find the words. I wanted to tell her of the peculiar stirrings that were occurring within me. As if I were emerging from a cocoon—a butterfly that was about to be born. I felt changed. I knew there would be time to tell all this and more. For now, it was my brother with whom we were all concerned.

It was on the second day after Lazarus had come home ill that the passing came. Martha rushed from his room and knelt beside my mother, taking her hand. "Mother, I believe Lazarus is going." With those words, her tears sprang anew, and we all went to his bedside.

Martha had administered the medicine earlier and Lazarus appeared peaceful, but the mask of death was light upon his face. My mother knelt beside him and held his hand and prayed. "Oh Lord! My son . . . my firstborn . . . if it is meant that he should live again, manifest Yourself to my dear one now . . . if it is meant that he should go to his heavenly home, may he go peacefully to his eternal rest."

Martha and I held one another and wept. Lazarus, thank God, was at peace. His breathing became shallow—and I could see that his soul or spirit had taken leave of the body. For it was as if he had shrunken in the bed since the day before. And although we were not able to find the Master, we knew that that night he would be coming to our home, at the invitation of my mother. By then, it would be too late—but I knew that the Master's presence would ease the broken heart of my mother and bring peace to the household.

As we stood at his bedside I found my voice, though choked with tears, and sang a psalm. My sister Martha joined me.

"God is our refuge and strength,
an ever-present help in trouble.

"Therefore we will not fear, though the earth give way
and the mountains fall into the heart of the sea,

"though its waters roar and foam
and the mountains quake with their surging.

"There is a river whose streams make glad the city of God,
the holy place where the Most High dwells.

"God is within her, she will not fall;
God will help her at break of day.

"Nations are in uproar, kingdoms fall;
he lifts his voice, the earth melts.

"The Lord Almighty is with us;
the God of Jacob is our fortress.

"Come and see the works of the Lord,
the desolations he has brought on the earth.

"He makes wars cease to the ends of the earth;

he breaks the bow and shatters the spear,
he burns the shields with fire.
    "'Be still, and know that I am God;
I will be exalted among the nations, I will be exalted in the earth.'
    "The Lord Almighty is with us;
the God of Jacob is our fortress. Selah"
    And with a breath and a sigh, my brother, Lazarus, took his flight
from this world, in a state of peace and grace. And we would feel great
Presences with us. Perhaps even though the Master could not be here,
he had sent his angels to bear my brother up. My mother stood and
embraced us.
    "There is nothing harder, my children," she said, her voice breaking,
"then to have to witness the death of your child." We wept together and
were quiet for a spell.
    "And yet," Martha said, "I know he lives. I can feel that his spirit is free
from these earthly confines—and although I shall miss him terribly—I
know he is fine—for he now walks with God."
    "Yes," I said, "I can feel that too. There was just so much I had yet to
tell him . . . so much I wanted to say . . . "
    My mother, wiser than I ever imagined her to be, said, "Then say
those things to him, for he has only shed the shell that held the soul—
the body. He will hear you. I cannot tell you how I know these things,
but I know them in my heart. It was love that we all shared—and that
bond of love cannot be broken—not even by death."
    "Still," I said, "I shall miss his voice, his touch, his presence with us."
    "Yes, that is the hardest part of the passing." My mother leaned over
the bed, tears streaming down her face and kissed her son's forehead.
"Peace be with you, my son. Now and always."
    We helped her out of his room and into her chair. My sister and I
would contact the rabbi and make arrangements for our brother's burial.
    It would be several days before the burial was to take place. We sent
messengers to distant family members and friends to tell them of my
brother's passing, and as is our custom, we did not disturb the body for
three days, after we had anointed him with spices and oils, and wrapped
the body in burial clothes. There was a hillside that was our family's
burial site—a large stone was rolled in front of the entry to the tomb.

We had Lazarus' body placed inside the tomb, until all the family, friends, and mourners had gathered. I was more than a little puzzled that I had not heard a word from the Master. Martha, too, wondered what could be keeping him. We had sent messengers and servants to all the places where he might visit and stay—still there was no word.

"Mary," Martha said. "Why has the Master not yet come? Could he have heard of Lazarus' death and turned back?"

"No," I said. "There is some good reason for his delay. But he will come."

"What faith you have, Mary! Do you ever doubt?"

"Not since I met the Master. I always pray for the faith of Job, who said, 'Though he slay me, yet will I trust in him.' I believe that the Master knows the will of the Father in Heaven and does it. This sorrow of ours must be for some perfect reason. I cannot understand it, but what would become of me if I should cease to believe on him?"

On the fourth day, the mourners were all gathered, my mother, and Martha and our friends went to the hillside where there would be the ceremony. Still I had my hopes that the Master would come. And my desire was not in vain. As we stood with the rabbi, I saw a small band of men coming to the funeral. My heart leapt within me and I grabbed Martha's hand. "It is he," I said. "The Master has come. As the Master drew closer with his Disciples, I told the rabbi to stay his words for a few moments. Mother, Martha, and I walked and met the Master.

The look upon his face was one that told me he felt everything that was within our hearts—our sorrow, our sense of loss—and that he too was saddened by the death of his friend. He came to my mother first, "Miriam, dear Miriam," and he held her tightly.

"Master," I heard her say to him, "had you been here my brother would not have died. We tried so long to find you."

After he embraced us all, the Master said. "It was for a reason that I was not present when he died." He looked deep into my eyes and then into Martha's.

"Your brother shall rise again," the Master said softly.

"Yes, I know he will rise again in the resurrection at the last day," my mother said.

"I am the resurrection and the life," said the Master. "He that believes on me, though he die, yet shall he live, and whoever lives and believes on me shall never die. Do you believe this, Martha?"

"Yes, Master," she replied. "I have believed that you are the Christ, the Son of God who should come into the world."

"Oh, Master!" I cried, falling at his feet, "I feel just like my mother. Had you been here, he would not have died." He lifted up and held me, and I felt his own tears, falling upon my shoulder. "Oh, dear child, I know your pain." He looked at Martha and my mother. "I know what you feel—for my heart beats with your own."

There were those who stood about us who exclaimed. "See how he loved him! He weeps!" Another person said, "Could not this man, who opened the eyes of the blind man, have kept his friend from death?"

I ignored the murmurings. The mourners were exclaiming among us—I felt that I was in a dream.

"Show me where he is buried," the Master said to me, and to Martha. He touched my mother's face and smiled. "Stay here, Mother Miriam."

We walked the short distance to the tomb.

He spoke to a group of men who had gathered at the funeral. "Take away the stone," the Master said.

"Master," Martha interrupted. "He has begun to rot—for he has been dead for four days."

"Did I not say unto you that if you believed, you would see the glory of God?" the Master asked.

Martha looked confused and backed away as the men rolled away the stone. I stood next to the Master even though the stench was nearly unbearable.

"Stand back, my child, and behold the glory of God," the Master said.

I walked back to my mother and Martha. We stood in silence. Many of those gathered backed away, covering their faces. And suddenly, everything stopped—there was complete stillness. I watched as the Master raised his right hand and look upward.

"Father," the Master said, "I thank thee that thou hast heard me. And I know that thou hearest me always, but because of the multitude which stand around, I said it, so that they may believe that thou didst send me. Glorify thy Son now, that Your power may be known among men."

After his prayer, he looked back at me and he smiled. In that moment my friends it was as if I were gazing into the eyes of God. No, I *knew* I was gazing into the eyes of God, made manifest in flesh.

And then the wind came. It came like a tempest—and it seemed to swirl about the Master. The crowd was uneasy and was now backing away from the Master. The mourners stopped uttering—their eyes transfixed upon the Master.

In a loud, booming voice, the Master cried:

"Lazarus, live again! Return to us!"

Suddenly, the bound figure of my brother appeared at the entrance of the tomb. My mother fainted and Martha caught her before she hit the ground. Some people were screaming and running away. The Master, completely unaware of the pandemonium, looked at John, the youngest Disciple and said, "Loosen him from the grave clothes and let him go."

John moved forward and unbound Lazarus, beginning at the head. When his face was revealed, his eyes were clear and alive. As John unbound him, Lazarus took several steps out of the tomb and looked at the Master, who was smiling. Lazarus ran to him and embraced him like a brother he had not seen in ages.

"Jesus, my friend," Lazarus said, "I was in the most glorious light, surrounded by angels and I and heard everything. It is like . . . there is no difference between life and death!"

"Life and death are one even as the river and sea are one," the Master said. "Welcome back."

Miriam was now sitting up with Martha. "Is it a dream?" she asked.

"No," Martha said. "Your son, who was dead, is alive again. Brought back by the Son of God."

Miriam rose from the ground, brushing the dust off of her clothes and went to her son. He looked as if had awoken from a nap—but was pink-cheeked, and healthy. She hugged her son and pulled the Master into the circle. "God be praised! My son has been returned to me. Master—how can I thank you? Lazarus, how are you feeling?"

The Master laughed. "Miriam, all glory and praise go to Him, the giver of all good and perfect gifts. Your son was brought back to life not by my will, but by God's will—a living demonstration of what was possible to show what human beings are capable of. And your son was returned to this world to show that with God, all things are possible."

"I feel hungry," Lazarus said. "I hope you prepare one of your banquets tonight, Mother." We all laughed and there was that feeling of being like children again.

"I will prepare the feast of feasts," Miriam exclaimed.

Martha's home is situated above the Mount of Olives, behind which lies Bethany, behind which the greatest miracle the world has ever known occurred—that my brother came back from the dead. That night, my mother and sister kept their promise—they held one of the greatest feasts I have ever known. Naturally, the conversation centered on what Lazarus recalled during the time that he was dead. He was perfectly frank about the experience.

"I do not remember any pain or suffering before I left the body," Lazarus said. "But I do remember feeling dreadful when I came into the house, and then it was as if I were watching all of you from far above—almost from the ceiling of the house. And I was filled with the most buoyant peace I have ever known. I remember being in the presence of the most loving light. And then, it seemed that I slept. The best way I can describe it is this—now that I have returned to this mortal realm," with this he smiled at the Master. "Have you not fallen asleep in the evening, and then in the morning awakened with the consciousness of having had some wondrous dream, but with no other recollection except that the dream was beyond all comparison marvelous? So it is with me. I fell asleep—you tell me—four days ago. The Master's voice roused me today. There was something wonderful in the interim. This is all I can tell you—except that it is only a thin veil that separates this world, from the realm of Spirit, and that I am glad to be here with you dear ones again." We all applauded.

When he concluded, there was silence, for we all wanted to hear what the Master would say. But he sat smiling as if waiting for one of us to speak. There is something in the Master's face that impresses me more and more—the more often I look upon it. As he sat there with that questioning smile, it was the face of a simple, loving man, who drew your heart to him as irresistibly as an affectionate child, and for the same reason—but when he stood before the tomb and cried, "Lazarus, live again!" his face was the face of God, and between these two extremes runs an infinity of expression which covers the whole range of human and even the superhuman.

One of the men gathered at the table, a Roman whom the Master had invited, said to the Master: "I formerly believed that our life ended with our breath, but now, since Lazarus has returned, I know that we are eternal. My motto was, as we Romans say, *Carpe diem.* Now I know we should live not so much for this life here on earth, as for the life to come—in heaven. Master, teach us of that life—for in that life, I suppose, we shall find the Kingdom you proclaim."

"No, Caius Claudius, you will not have to wait for that life to behold the Kingdom—for the Kingdom of Heaven is within you, here and now, and, just as you open your eyes in the morning and behold the light of the sun, so you only need to open the eyes of your heart to behold the Kingdom of Heaven in all its glory."

The Master then went on to detail more of the Kingdom, which I will tell at a later time. For now, because the hour draws late, I must finish the story of my dear brother Lazarus. I wish I could say that it has a happy ending—but my friends, it is rather sad I am afraid to say.

After the feast, an immense crowd came out of Jerusalem to Bethany, for the news of raising Lazarus had spread quickly, and people were curious to see what a resurrected man looked like, and if it were possible to hear his experiences. He told them about the glorious Light, and that the life we live here continues on, but beyond that, the crowd was disappointed that he could not tell them more of his experience. At the same time many sick people were brought out, and when the Master returned from prayer he healed them all. Some of those who crowded about him and touched the hem of his garment were healed without a word being spoken! It is marvelous what power resides in this man, and it came from nowhere but God, who has made and preserves all things.

I was uneasy—for behind the believers stood prominent Pharisees and Sadducees, members of the Sanhedrin. They stood aloof and seemed to conspire and consult with one another in whispers. They kept pointing at the Master and at Lazarus. I did not like their attitude, so I sent several servants to find out what they were saying. When they returned I was more upset than ever. For the servants overheard them saying that the Master's miracles were by the power of Beelzebub in order to mislead the people of Israel, that no true prophet would act as a physician on the Sabbath and break other ordinances, as the Master did. They also said that if the Master continued his wicked course, some great evil would befall God's temple and the people. For the first time I began to fear for the Master's safety in the midst of such bitter enemies.

When the Master went alone to pray, I waited upon him. And after an hour, he saw me standing near an olive grove and I shared with him the knowledge I had gained.

"Dear Mary," he said. "My time is not yet. The vipers may set their traps, and say that I work from evil designs or forces, but fear not. Remember, your brother walks again among you. And you are a changed woman!" With these words he smiled that smile I learned to love so well. But in his eyes I saw a sadness I could not place, as if he were looking ahead at something coming in the future, and without any expression of fear, there was that tinge of sadness. As quickly as the look in his eye came, it passed, and he again turned his attention to me.

"It is not of myself that I do these things, Mary. I follow the promptings of God that speaks to us through the heart. What He bids me to do, I must do. All people have this ability, this connection with the Unseen God, and I have come into the earth to show mankind that God does not speak through sacrifice or stone temples, but through the human heart. And if you take time to listen, He will speak with you. You are His child, a glorious, eternal creation brought into being for eternity, but to walk upon the earth only for a moment in time. Eventually, the day will arrive when all people shall do the things I have demonstrated. Turn within, Mary, look deeply within your heart and contemplate God there, in the silence. All that I have learned in my travels, in my education has taught me that one thing—The Creator is a God of Spirit, and desires us to worship Him in Spirit. Until that message is shared and taken to heart by many, many people, my work is not yet finished. So do not fear for my safety."

My fears were allayed for only a short time, for the Master's time was much shorter than I realized. But he, in his kindness, did not want me to worry over him. Neither did he tell me of the fate of my brother Lazarus. Though he was brought back from the dead—he only lived among us for a short time. I did not know it at the time, but the Roman and religious authorities saw Jesus as the enemy. And so many people had heard of Lazarus and what had happened on that glorious day when he was resurrected from death, it was only a matter of time before the dark ones would conspire against him. For wherever my brother went he was thronged about by masses of people. Naturally, people wanted to know what death was like—and he was a living miracle among us . . . for only a short season.

The Romans assassinated my brother on a day when he was in the marketplace in Jerusalem. We still to this day do not know who killed him, but we know why. Lazarus was living proof that Jesus was the Messiah—for the Master represented Life and spoke unto Death, and Death gave up its hold upon my brother.

Neither the Romans nor the Sanhedrin could afford to have my brother walking around. They stabbed him when the throngs of people were pressing against him to hear him tell the tale once again of his journey on the Other Side of this life. I was not there when it happened—neither was the Master nor any of the family. We received word from a kindly messenger that Lazarus had been stabbed to death in the marketplace outside Jerusalem.

Though we lost him to death twice, we had the privilege, thanks be to God through the Master, to have him live and laugh among us again for a season. I know now that he lives—yes, unencumbered by the limitations of this physical body. I have no doubt that he will be there for me, when my time comes to cross that bridge to the Other Side of Life.

3

On Mary,
the Mother of Jesus

I was still upon the threshold of shedding my worldly self when the Master gave me one of the most precious gifts of all: His mother. At the time that he came to my home to find me, my sister was busying herself—as usual—and she saw Jesus coming up the road. For the first time in many days, he was alone—without the throngs of hangers-on who sought a healing or wanted to touch his garment or just be near him. It was passing strange to see him walking alone.

"Mary!" Martha cried, "Jesus is coming here. Get up, help me get the house in order." I had seen the Master coming even before my sister, and my heart was full with his arrival, and I didn't care if our home was a hovel—like the Master, I was not one to deal in appearances. I looked at my sister and walked past her much to her protesting.

Seeing that it was he, Jesus, walking to our home, I again

felt like he was the oasis from which I could quench a thirst that I could not define. Just the vision of him filled the part of me I did not know was empty . . . until I saw him. I know now it was my yearning for his spirit—for the spirit of God—and nothing in this material world would ever satisfy that longing. I could not wait on the porch, so I walked down the road toward him, trying desperately not to run. He smiled at me as he saw me, and all at once I again felt like a small child, almost shy (I was not known to be shy in those days), but his smile could make me blush. Walking with him . . . how can I find the words for such an experience? There are none, but I must try. For whoever finds these pages in the days, years, centuries after I am gone, I want them to be able to *feel* the Master as I did. So I will do my best (a feeble attempt to be sure), to bring back the days in which I walked with him in the sun and in the moonlight, and explain what the experience was like when I walked, side-by-side—with the Son of God. I only pray that these pages find their way into the hands of a compassionate soul, one who knows that this record is of my own hand, Mary of Magdalene, and all that I write here is true to the best of my memory. At this point in my life, I have nothing to lose—I only pray there will be time to write all that I can recall.

In the moment I wrote those words, I had a flashing vision of the man who would find the parchments—many, many years in the future—and he will be one of us. One of those of whom the Master called "the generation that shall not pass until all these things are fulfilled." A blessed reassurance—and I know it has come from him, the Master.

To return to the story of the Master's coming to my home. While Martha busied herself in getting the house ready, I knew in my heart that Jesus had no intention of entering in. I do not know how I knew this, but I knew. There was something in his eyes—those beautiful steel blue-gray eyes. When we met upon the road, he took my hands in his.

"Mary," he said. Just that. My name. Suddenly, tears ran like rivers down my cheek and I threw my arms around him, completely unaware if anyone might see me—and disapprove. The Master and I shared a common bond: People will say what they will about you. They will talk behind your back and say what they will—true or untrue. I was blessed with the gift of not caring one iota for either. The Master illustrated this

principle many times in many stories—sometimes in front of the pre-
tentious Pharisees, who prayed long and loud in the streets only to be
heard by the people, not by God.

"When you pray," the Master said on more than one occasion, "pray
in secret. The hypocrites pray loud and long in front of adoring throngs.
They have their reward there and then. However, those who pray in
secret, their reward will be received on that Other Shore, after this life is
over. An unselfish prayer spoken from the heart can lift a soul from
despair into the Light. Yea, a handful of the faithful quietly praying and
meditating for peace can save nations from destruction. So pray to the
Father–Mother–God in quiet groups, or alone—but know that your
prayers, spoken from the heart, will be heard. That is the key: *From the
heart.*"

All of this ran through my mind as he held me in his loving embrace—and I cannot describe it any other way except . . . I was home—
home. This was the word that kept echoing through my mind as he held
me. And I knew not from where my tears came. Except that sometimes
when the soul is so filled with love the only way it can express itself,
give voice to the ecstasy it feels within itself is through tears. The Master
must have known this, for he did not ask, "Mary, what is the matter?" He
knew that my feelings were too vast for words.

As he had done any times before, he seemed to read my thoughts.

"You long for home—a home that is far away from the troubles of this
earth," the Master said.

"I long to be *changed,*" I said. "For there are times where my heart is
not tamed, where I feel the old demons of my old life coming back to
haunt me. Master, I am haunted by what I once was, what I once did
. . . how can you even look upon me without judgment or—even when
we walk in the streets, you hold your head high to be seen with me . . .
me!" I could barely get the words out for my voice was choked with
tears.

"Mary, Mary," he said, holding me closer still. "The Creator and I love
every thing about you that you consider unlovable! You are now and
ever shall be the Lady of Mystery—the Woman with Heart—the woman
I chose among all others to be with me upon this journey. It is because
you have seen the world, and loved in the world. It is because you have

always had something burning, yearning in your heart for something . . .
Someone . . . to show you the way."

With this, my tears overflowing with gratitude and a love too vast to
put into words, he, the Master, looked at me. And said, "I am that Something. I am that Someone that you longed for. And the yearning is not
of the physical flesh, no, but it is deeper than that. It is the part of you
that is the part of God, longing for Home—the Spiritual Home."

With that he took my face in his hands and smiled upon me, and he
laughed, kissing away the tears on my face. As he did there was something in me that I felt was changed, transformed in some mysterious
way I cannot describe.

The Master then put his hands upon my head and said a prayer in a
language I was not familiar with. From his hands there was a great heat,
and I felt the residue of my old self, departing. It was as if I were standing in a place of light and shadow. The shadows departed from me and
I knew these were the things I had held onto from my old former self:
selfishness, lust, avarice—those which are known as the seven deadly
sins. To this day and for the rest of my life I can see them taking flight—
they were hideous forms coming out of me in all directions. Shadow-
like forms that came out of me, all the while the Master prayed. I threw
back my head and felt a scream rising from me. Not one of terror, no,
but one of great relief, as if part of me was dying and yet being replaced
with something else. I thought I was changed when the Master first
saved me from the stoning pit, but no. That was only the first step.
Before then . . . I was a woman lost to the world, a slave to my passions,
to my lovers, to the world of material things. No, I cannot even say
lovers—for they were not. They did not love me—only the physical shell
that my soul inhabits.

Gone from me were also the feelings of guilt and remorse of the
person I had been. I would have collapsed in that moment had it not
been for the Master, who gently held me, like a child. He held me like
the ocean holds a wave—and I felt as if I were home.

Again I looked into the Master's eyes and whispered the words that
I had never said to any man.

"I love you."

He smiled and all that was night in me was made daylight. Looking into his eyes—again there was the feeling of coming home.

"I love you, too, Mary," he said. "In the past men have pretended to love you only for yourself. I alone love the unseen in you."

In that moment was when a change came in me. I recognized myself not as Mary of Magdalene, a body of flesh, but as a being of light—belonging to something greater than the world . . . I had never felt God so fully before in my life. I felt as if I were dying and yet being born.

"Come with me," he said. "I know your heart—and I know your longings. You are in a state of *becoming.*" That's the word the Master used—"becoming."

"Is that what is happening to me? I don't know what that means."

"You are becoming acquainted with your soul again. That is one of the reasons I have come into the world. To show mankind that they are more than a house of flesh—but that all can be reborn in the Spirit. What you just felt were the layers of your old self—not the real Self—but the Mary that has known only the world, dying. This process is like the caterpillar emerging from its cocoon to become the butterfly."

I pondered his words. "Still, there are times where I can feel the demons that I thought were gone from me."

"Mary, they are only shadows of the past," he said. His voice—his words were my salvation. I could feel the reassurance—the *truth* of his words flowing over me like sacred water. I do not know if it was his touch, or his words—but they banished the feelings of restlessness, and my soul was quiet, at peace.

"Come with me, "he said, "I want you to counsel with my mother—there is much that she can tell you that will help you understand many things."

I went with the Master to his mother's home in the hills of Nazareth. She was a woman of infinite beauty and kindness. As she opened the door, it was as if she had been waiting for me to arrive and she welcomed me with love in her heart. For this, I was grateful—for though I had renounced my former life, I knew that there were stories that were told of me, about me, throughout the land of Judea. I was foolish to think that there might be some judgment in this woman concerning me. Looking back on that, I can see how ridiculous that was—for this was the Mother of the Master! As I gazed into her blue eyes, I could feel the love—complete and unconditional—for me, though we had never met. Again, there was the feeling of coming home.

"Welcome, dear Mary," she said, and embraced me like a long lost daughter. Then she turned her gaze to her son and there was a mixture of joy and sadness in her blue eyes. She appeared younger than I had anticipated. The Master and his mother physically looked so close in age I thought they could be brother and sister.

"Jesus," she said. He came to her waiting arms with that brilliant smile. "Mother," he said.

"You have brought to me another of your Disciples," Mary said, and my heart nearly stopped beating! A Disciple? Me? There was a twinkle in her eye, and she smiled upon me. I do not have words to express the feelings of joy that filled me.

"Yes, Mother," he said, "She is numbered amongst the ones I have chosen. And she has chosen me." Tears welled up in my eyes. I could barely find the words to speak.

Though there were husks in my throat, and my tears were near to overflowing, I managed to say, "I am honored to be in your home."

"My dear, all are welcome here," Mary said. "Come. Sit with me. There is much we have to talk about."

In my mind, I felt as if I had known this beautiful woman for . . . always. It was the same feeling I had when the Master had saved me from my death.

"Jesus, will you be staying?" Mary asked.

"No, I must be about the Father's business."

Upon hearing this, Mary laughed and said to me, "This is what my son said to me when he was ten years old. We had gone to Jerusalem on a buying trip and he disappeared. We searched and searched and could not find him. It wasn't until the next day we found him in the Temple, discussing and arguing with the priests! At ten years of age!" She nudged her son lovingly and he lowered his head, laughing quietly at the memory.

"When my husband, Joseph and I, finally found him and asked him where he had been—that we were worried almost to illness over his disappearance, he looked at us impatiently and said—

"I must be about the Father's business," Jesus answered before his mother could, still laughing.

"Ah, my son, my son," Mary said, smiling and holding him in an embrace. Then her face and the tone of her voice became somber. "Please be careful where you travel. I have heard stories from some of the women that you are stirring up some trouble out there. I try not to worry but as a mother—"

Jesus interrupted her. "Mother, my time is not yet fulfilled. There is much yet the people need to hear. Know that His angels have charge over me."

She looked at me, and again there was an indefinable sadness in her eyes. "He is my son, and yet not my son. He was born of me, but his Spirit has come from the stars, from the heavens—and he belongs to all."

"I love you, Mother," Jesus said, kissing her good-bye.

"And you know my love for you," Mary said. "Godspeed, my son."

The Master then leaned over to me and with a kiss upon my cheek he said he would return to bring me home at twilight. "Tell her all, Mother," Jesus said as he walked out the door. As he departed, I had the strange feeling that Mary and her son were *one*—I cannot describe the feeling another way. I felt as if they were two halves of one soul. I understand more now than I did then.

As I went to the door to watch Jesus depart from his mother's home, I looked upon the road and he was gone! As if he had vanished into the very air itself. I stepped out of the door and he had disappeared like a phantom.

Mary was not looking at the road, but at me, smiling. "As I said, my dear, he is of the stars and the heavens, and holds dominion even over them. For his mind has become one with the Creator's. His personality is the son I gave birth to, but his spirit—it is infinite and entwined and at one with the Creator. You must know this, for you are the sister of Lazarus are you not?"

"Yes, my lady, I am," I said, almost bowing before her.

"Please, call me Mary," she said. In my heart I wanted so much to call her 'Mother'—for her countenance was . . . was simply what I have come to know as 'The Mother of all.' How close to the truth I was! But at the time, I did not know.

She led me to a beautiful room, decorated with tapestries from Persia. There were statues from India and linen draperies from Egypt. I felt this was a sacred room—a place where one could reflect and pray—for the essence of God seemed to emanate from the very walls of Mary's home itself.

"My son has traveled to many lands," Mary said. "And he brought me these gifts upon his return. My son has been educated in all of the places you have just thought of—India, Persia, and Egypt."

After all that I had seen and heard from spending time with the Master I was not surprised that Jesus' Mother could read my thoughts as clearly as one could hear the sound of my voice. It was a strange way of *knowing* that this was so—and I was not intimidated or made shy by her ability. For I knew that, like her Son, she saw each person from the heart. As the Master had taught, at the heart of every individual is the Center of God within. I felt closer to her than ever before.

There were others in the house. A woman named Matada brought us tea and bread, and Mary introduced us. She was shy but very courteous. After she departed the house became quiet and I sat in a comfortable chair across from Mary. She poured tea in Oriental cups and then she began to speak as she handed me my cup.

Her parents were Joachim and Anna. Her father was a man of Jewish law and her mother, Anna, was of the tribe of Judah. She was born into a Jewish sect known as the Essenes, also known as "The Expectant Ones."

"I was very young in years when my mother and father took me to the School of the Prophets," Mary said, and quickly added with a laugh, "No, I am not a prophet. However, my parents told the Elders of the temple at Mount Carmel, where the School had been established since time immemorial, that my birth was a miraculous one. My mother was beyond her childbearing years and she told the Elders that there had been no intimacy between her and my father. That she was with child, well, it was inexplicable." Mary gazed at me and added, "I know how incredible that may sound."

"My brother Lazarus walks and talks with people of every clime about his journey to the Other World, Mary," I said. "He had been dead for four days when your beloved son came to us. After that experience, these things are not difficult to believe. I marvel at them, oh yes! But I doubt no more—my mind is open and even the change in my own self is nothing short of a miracle. I do not doubt anything you say. Your son has not only opened my eyes, but my mind, my heart, and my spirit. Since the day that he saved me, my mind will not turn anywhere but toward him, the Master, your son."

She smiled. "Yes, Mary, it was my son, but my son is but the vessel which God uses to manifest things—miracles—to show mankind what is possible when the heart, the body, the mind and soul are made one with God. For God does not only reside in the outer world, but in here." She put her hand to her heart. "There are times when it is beyond the fathoms to believe that this man of God came through me." She shook her head in humbleness.

I was bold enough to place my hand upon hers and said, "Except for rare moments, I am now at peace—what he calls the 'peace that passes all understanding.' My delight is to wait upon him, to minister to his wants. And I thank God that he has given me the strength to overcome all that I have and removed the veil from my vision. And I can see that he, your son, is the Holy One who has come to set us free and break down the illusion that we are separate from God. I know he is a man, but I also know that his voice is the Voice of God. You are blessed, Mary, for being chosen to be his mother. You gave birth to a sacred legacy that has been destined and prophesied since the writing of the Sacred Books. You shall be remembered and honored until the end of time. I know your son is the Messiah." The tears that I had tried to hold back earlier now spilled down my cheeks.

Tears also filled Mary's eyes and she placed her other hand upon mine. "Bless you, dear Mary. I never dreamed that the One, my son, would be born unto me. After spending years in the temple service, from age three onward—being trained and disciplined in that sacred school—and it was not an easy childhood—but I grew to have mastery over my desires, and I learned to still my mind to listen for the great Silence, the sacred Voice of God—I was astonished when I was visited by the great Archangel Gabriel." Her voice was silent for a moment and in her eyes there was still awe and wonder at the great happening.

"What did the angel say to you?" I asked.

Mary looked deep into my eyes and tears spilled over cheeks and her voice quivered. "I was leading the other eleven girls who were going through the initiation with me, up the temple steps. It was a glorious morning—everything was bathed in purple and gold as the sun rose. Suddenly, there was a clap of thunder and everyone except me fell to the ground upon their knees—some lay completely on the ground but I could not move. I saw a great light coming from the heavens. For a moment I was afraid, and then the light shone down upon me and all fear was gone. I was bathed in a Sacred Light. I saw a great white being, infinitely kind but mighty—oh how mighty was this angel! In his hand he carried a white lily and took me by the hand and led me to the altar where we prayed every morning. Mary, I cannot describe to you how I felt when I heard the words of the angel. "God has found favor with you, Mary. You shall be called blessed by all nations for you shall bear a son, Immanuel, the Chosen One of God, who shall set all men free. Blessed art thou amongst women."

Mary wept at the memory. I held her hands tightly. In my mind I could see all that she described and I silently thanked God that I had gone through everything I had been through to arrive at this wonderful, glorious moment in time.

"Oh, Mary," was all I managed to say, exclaiming my own awe and wonder and joy.

"Forgive me my tears," she said, "they are tears of joy." I felt her hands tighten in my own. "I was thirteen years old when this . . . this miracle happened," she said. "I remember little else of that day, for I was in a state of ecstasy for a long time afterward. But I do remember, after the light and the great angel receded, that I was kneeling *upon* the altar. We always knelt in front of the altar, but no one, except the Elders ever touched the sacred altar or placed flowers or sacred objects upon it. I can remember there was a glorious sound coming from the people all around me. There were hands touching me and they carried me to my little room.

"The Elder who was in charge of us, Judy, came to my room some time afterwards and I told her what the angel had said. She wept. She said, 'For three hundred years we have been raising girls in this School of the Prophets, from age three until they reached the age of seventeen. It has been the Sacred Purpose and desire of all of the Essenes that one day, God would choose one of the girls to bring the Messiah into the earth. You have been chosen, Mary.'"

Mary dabbed her eyes with a linen cloth, looked at me, and smiled. "I was astonished beyond belief. I wondered how this could come to be, since I was just a girl. 'As God has sent the Angel of Annunciation to you, God will guide you the rest of the way,' Judy said. She hugged me and for the next three years I dedicated myself in service to the Essene community. I prayed and meditated and began to hear the Voice of the Great Angel and what I felt was the voice of God—if I may be so bold to say so. And always the message was, 'All is well, be not afraid, peace be with you.' When I was sixteen years of age, I was still in the Temple service, and I awoke one morning to see the same light I had seen at the altar shining through my window. It was shining upon the lower half of my body and I felt warmth and something *alive* leapt within me. I lay again in ecstasy, and when I did not make it to the sunrise prayer period, that is the way the Elders found me—lying prone upon my bed with the Light shining down upon me. Many said that they saw angels in the Light, coming to and fro, to and fro, upwards into the heavens and down into my room and going through my body. Again, I remember little of this, only the feeling and the knowing, the clear knowing that what was promised to me three years earlier was going to come to pass."

Again I was so filled with wonder and the Spirit that I could not find words to speak. Just as with the Master, when he spoke, I could see images unfolding in my mind, I could see all—everything—that Mary told me. It was as if I experienced it with her. She told me that as the months passed, it was clear to all that she was with child—and yet she was still a virgin. How wondrous and marvelous are the works of God! I was astonished at the faith of the Essenes—the tiny sect that believed what the prophets of old had said: That one day, God would come to the earth and dwell amongst men and show all the way.

She told me that her being with child, and without a husband, was to be kept secret—to be held within the confines of the community. When the time came for the birth that too would be a secret. They now looked to Mary for direction, whereas before she had looked to the Elders. They were afraid of Herod the Great, and Caesar Augustus—and what they would do if they found out about Mary's condition.

At last, just several months before there was to be the birth, the worst thing that the Essenes could conceive of happened.

"Word of my condition spread," Mary said. "We do not know how or by whom—but rumors were circulating throughout Judea about the young girl who was with child, and without husband. The Elders and I went into deep prayer and meditation, for we did not know what to do. The Divine Direction was given that there was a man who followed closely with God and was from the house of Judah—the man who would eventually become my husband, Joseph. I had met him in social gatherings and he was open to the tenets of the Essenes, although many sects of the Jewish community were not. When the Elders and I met with him and told him the story I have shared with you, Mary, he was more than a little confounded! He did not at first believe—and I did not blame him. The story seems too incredible to be true! But Judy told me that he would have a visitation, either in a dream or in his prayer period that would convert his heart to the truth of the story.

"The very next day," Mary continued, "Joseph came to our temple worship and took me by the hand. What Judy had proclaimed was true, a great angel called the Lord of the Way, the great Archangel Michael, visited Joseph in a dream and told him that all he had heard was true, and that it was a Divine Ordinance that he was to be wed to me, and that the son I would bear would become the Messiah, the first perfect expression of God–Man made manifest in flesh."

Mary said that the announcement of the wedding was spread throughout the land and she and Joseph were married by one of the Essene ministers. "I have loved him since the day I saw him," Mary said.

I knew that Jesus' mother had a cousin Elizabeth and they were a very close family. At the same time that Mary gave birth to Jesus, Mary said, her cousin Elizabeth also gave birth to a son named John. She too had a visitation from an angel and was told that the two, Jesus and John, would be together through childhood, and that John would become the Forerunner, the one who would announce, when the time was ready, that Jesus was the One that had been foretold by the prophets of old.

"My son was born in a place of hiding outside of Bethlehem," Mary said. "We had to make the long trek from Nazareth to Bethlehem to register for the tax. I was so close to giving birth to Jesus I wondered if it would happen on the journey! We traveled with a band of the Essenes who went before us and after us heading toward Bethlehem. Judy, with her gift of vision, went into deep prayer and meditation and was able to check on our progress from Mount Carmel. We were told to go to a specific inn in Bethlehem and the innkeeper would direct us where we would go."

Mary laughed at the memory. "The innkeeper put on a good appearance for us, and for those who were drinking and carousing at the inn. 'We have no room here!' He shouted above the noisiness of the place. Some were pointing at us and laughing for Joseph was twenty years older than I. Here I was, a girl of sixteen! As soon as we stepped back outside, the innkeeper's daughter, Susanna, a wonderful girl, came and took us to a safe place—it was a cave-like dwelling inset upon a hill, far from the rowdiness of the crowd. They had made the place as comfortable as possible for us. Oh, it was an amazing night, Mary, the night my son was born. The birthing was easy and we had the aid of one of the Essenes who acted as the midwife. At the stroke of midnight, Jesus, my son, was born."

Mary bowed her head in remembrance of that night. Very quietly she said, "There were angels, Mary. Choirs of angels that everyone heard when Jesus was born—they were singing! The most beautiful music you've ever heard. The heavenly music even quieted the inn. Not a sound was heard when I took my last deep breath, and Jesus came into the world. I could see, where I was lying, the North Star, and I knew that my son was imminent when the light of the North Star filled the cave-like dwelling with light!" Again, Mary wiped away a tear and she never took her hands from mine. It was as if she was transferring all that had happened to her to my heart, my mind, and my soul. Even now, I can hear her voice speaking to me.

"Could you hear what the angels were singing, Mary?" I asked.

"Oh yes!" she exclaimed. "It was wonderful, just beautiful. 'Peace! Peace on earth to all people of good will and good faith!'"

"What was it like to hold him in your arms?" I astonished myself by asking the question. Mary looked at me with complete seriousness and the wonder still filled her eyes.

"I have no words for that moment," she said. "Joseph was in tears, as was the midwife. And dear Susanna, who had prepared this wonderful place for Jesus' birth, was the first to hold him, after Joseph and I. And the light of the North Star continued to shine and give us warmth on that blessed night."

I moved over from where I sitting so I could sit next to Mary. I've never felt such a bond between another woman and myself in such a powerful way. I felt that she was the Mother of All. She had given birth to the first perfected soul—complete perfection.

"And it was promised to me," Mary said, "that what has happened to me will happen to other women in the times, the generations to come." I took her words into my heart and held them close. I can't put into words the astonishment I felt.

"You mean—?"

Mary interrupted me and said, "Yes, I and my son are the first of many. What I have done, it is destined that other women will do likewise. What my son is doing, one day, all men will do. They will cure the sick, the halt, and the lame. They will even raise people from the dead, as your brother was raised, when it is Divinely ordained."

Mary told me that it was decided by the Elders of the Essene Community that Jesus should begin his Sacred Education under the learned Masters in the East—Persia, India, and finally Egypt. He would depart with Judy at age ten. Before he reached that age, Mary said her son was a very playful child—a boisterous boy, daring and adventurous—but that he also demonstrated powers of healing from a very young age.

"He was like every other boy," Mary said, "but we knew that he was special from the time he began to walk and then run, and play with other children. I remember him playing with a little boy who was seriously ill. The boy, his mother said, did not have long to live—he had some sort of blood condition that the physicians could not heal. While playing with Jesus—I think the boy was five at the time—my son brushed a leaf out of the boy's hair. As soon as he touched his hair, the color came back to the little boy's cheeks, the weight he had lost was suddenly restored, and he and Jesus were laughing and laughing. I watched this happen from the back window where I could keep an eye on them and I knew in my heart that in that moment the little boy was healed! He ran home after playing with my son and later that night his mother came to call—and she was in tears. There was no sign of illness in the boy, and his appetite had returned to normal. Mary said she asked Jesus about what had happened with the boy being well and in a very matter of fact way of speaking Jesus said, "Oh, God made him feel better, I just brushed the leaf out of his hair."

Today that little boy is named Levi, and he is a close friend and follower of my son," Mary said.

After Jesus went off to school, Joseph and Mary had three more children, Ruth, James, and Jude. Ruth, she said, had the hardest time believing all the stories she heard surrounding the birth of Jesus.

"Ruth was the most level-headed child you'd ever meet," Mary said. "She would ask me all kinds of questions. Questions about the angel at the altar, and how it was possible for Jesus to be born without having a human father. She just couldn't believe such a thing was possible. For many years she didn't believe any of it—and I didn't interfere with her beliefs, nor did her father. James and Jude didn't talk to me about it all until they were older. The turning point in Ruth's life came just recently."

"When?" I asked.

"When Jesus was at the tomb of your brother, Lazarus," Mary said, "Ruth was there at the funeral. She witnessed it all."

I sat there, amazed at myself that I was having conversations with Mary, the mother of Jesus. She was so kind, and very humble about the miraculous events of her life. She always gave credit to God. And she seemed as astonished as I was about it all!

Many other things Mary said to me, but the ink runs low, as does the parchment—and I will write more of what she told me, and events in the life of the Master. In closing this portion of the diary, I shall never forget her words, about herself, and about her son and the future: "We are the first of many who will do what God has made manifest in our lives. God has ordained that a new race will come into being and there will, one day, be a heaven on earth. It may be ten thousand years from now, but one day, all will be redeemed—and what my son is now doing, others will do just like him. For all people have God within them. It is only a matter of letting God take the helm of the person's life."

4

The Wedding Feast at Cana

I awoke last night from a dream, although it seemed like a vision and not a dream. When the Master said, "I am with you always—I am with you all days," this was a literal promise—not a parable, or mere words to give us comfort when the dark days would come, when those of the Darkness would come and attempt to extinguish the Light the Master gave to us.

In my dream-vision, I saw him. And knowing it was him, I ran through a beautiful field—a place more beautiful than can be found in this world. I called out to him and he ran to me. Imagine running to reunite with the love of your life— and that poor description is the closest I can describe. For he was—and is—the love of my life—and until time is no more— he always will be. Do not misinterpret my words—before I met the Master, I had many lovers, and even after I met him there were some that I saw from time to time. I am not ashamed to say this because that was the old self, the worldly Mary, who he, the Master, set free. As I may have said, being near to him, was being in love to such a degree that it far surpassed any earthly romance or passion. He *was* romance—he *was* passion—he was Love Incarnate.

In the presence of such Love, the lovers I had known before fell away from me like the leaves in Autumn. The times that he would embrace me, or touch my face, or my hair, or hold my hand, I knew I was being touched and held by the living Christ—the Messiah—the One the prophets from old foretold would come and dwell among us. How short-sighted were the church elders, the keepers of the ancient sacred writings! They interpreted that the Messiah would come in a golden chariot, with a scepter and a crown—and that he would set up his kingdom.

But when he came, he came as a man not unlike you and me. Perhaps it was easier for me to believe because I bore witness to the ordinariness of Him—and yet at the same time, I was witness to the extraordinariness that he brought to a dying world. Although the church leaders were witness to the healings, and listened to the simple message that "love is what matters, and to love your neighbor as yourself, and to forgive your enemies—for even they have the spark of God within them"—they believed not.

"Your Father in Heaven cannot forgive you," the Master once said, "if you do not forgive. This is a law. All things—thoughts and deeds—will return to you. Your prophets have said, 'An eye for an eye, a tooth for a tooth.' And many misinterpreted this to mean that if one causes another—taking an eye—then it is well to take an eye from the one who caused the first transgression. But there is a larger truth here, and it is also written in the Scriptures: Those who take up the sword, shall die by it. In the sight of the Heavenly Father-Mother-God, all things done in the body must be met in the body—in this time or in the future. So, the larger truth is this: If you take an eye, you shall give an eye."

It should be no surprise that this did not sit well with the Pharisees, and it stirred up many in the crowds. The Master knew their thoughts, and added: "By the same token, those who sow from the heart seeds of love, then it is love that will be reaped. That which you sow, my friends, is what you shall reap. Sow your seed wisely, for you shall one day inherit the harvest."

Is it any wonder that the Master's teachings caused a dual reaction in so many people? The Master called this law the Eternal Balance of Recompense. He also said, "You rightly say, when someone passes from this world into the next after death, 'They have gone to their reward.' What *is* their reward? It is not of importance whether they were 'good or bad.' What waits for man on the Other Side is created by both deeds and thoughts—and most importantly by the *intent behind the deed*. Do not be deceived: follow your heart, and the dictates of your conscience—irrespective of 'what will people think?' For, while mankind looks upon the outward appearance, God looks upon the heart. If love is the motivating factor behind what you do, then you are laying up your treasures in heaven. As a consequence, if the motivating force behind your deeds is, 'people will think highly of me . . . I will be in good favor with the church if I give this or that,' then you already have earned your reward. Therefore, lay up for yourselves treasure in heaven, not on earth. For all that is of the earth passes away, but the spirit of goodness, of charity, of kindness, of compassion, and, yes, forgiveness of your enemies, these live on with you after you pass from this mortal plane, and create goodness in the souls of those not yet born."

In the dream, all of the Master's words came back to me—but there was more. All of the experiences, the best of our experiences were projected upon the sky in front of us. It was as if part of me was watching it, while at the same time I was experiencing it all. I was in awe and all around us—everywhere I looked, was the all-too-short period of time I had with the Master. We both sat upon the hillside and he was in a joyous mood—or perhaps I should say he *was* the Joyous Mood. For in the Master's presence, you *became* a part of his awareness, his emotions. And even in the darkest hours, he remained a tower of strength to us all, reminding us that the earthly life is but a fleeting one. In the fleeting moment we are upon this earth, he taught us to see the Spirit of the Unseen God in all that we meet. In so doing, he said, the soul is lifted from its petty concerns, it is lifted to the place of Love Divine. Hearing those words from him, I could believe—and I never had a day where I felt low or alone after he told me such.

"Is there something you would like to see, Mary?" the Master asked.

I opened my mouth but was speechless—he put his arm around me. I felt waves of love and such indescribable joy—it simply was beyond words. When I did find my voice, I said, "Yes, Master, I want to see the wedding feast at Cana. For I know there was much that went on that I was not aware of at the time of the feast." This was the time, although it is much disputed to this day, when the Master turned water into the finest wine I have ever tasted. It was a joyous occasion. And in this beautiful place—I wanted to remember one of the most wonderful evenings I spent with him.

When I gave the Master my request, he smiled and nodded, and he passed his hand in the sky and suddenly I was watching the Master as a small boy, perhaps eight or ten years of age. He and his Mother, Mary, and Joseph were riding on donkeys through what appeared to be desert terrain.

"So that you fully understand, Mary," the Master said, "I must show you what went on before."

As the scene unfolded, I saw the Master, as a child, and he was traveling with his Mother and Father on a desert road, where—when they came across a caravan or a house and asked for food or drink, they were always turned away. I could see the anxiousness in the face of Mary, for she was more afraid for her son than for herself. The Holy Family seemed to be traveling with many people — in front and behind—as if they were being guarded and protected upon the journey. I could see from the appearance that all were tired to the depths of their very beings.

"What is this I am seeing?" I quietly asked.

"This was the return from Egypt back to the land of my birth," the Master said.

I knew, from later conversations with the Master's mother, that, after she gave birth in Bethlehem, Herod had ordered the death of all children—ages two years and under. For he had heard from many that the Messiah had been born. In his ignorance and cruelty, he ordered his soldiers to kill all the babies in the land of Judea—all male children age two years and under. This was how desperate Herod was in his attempt to take the life of the One who was destined to become the Messiah. But

Joseph had a dream several nights before the terrible edict was issued. Archangel Michael came to him in a dream and said to take the child to Egypt—for there would be refuge and safety. The family obeyed and dwelt in Egypt for some eight years, until Herod died.

I wondered what all this had to do with the wonderful night of the wedding feast in Cana, near Capernum.

"Joseph," Mary said in this vision, "we must find food and water." She looked very anxious and worried. She held her son closer to her as they slowed to a stop to rest.

"The Lord has guided us safely to Egypt to escape from Herod," Joseph said, "and I know that He will see us safely home again."

At once the boy, Jesus, spoke up and said, "Mother, do not worry. I know where there is food and water." Mary looked into the eyes of her son.

"And where, my dear one, is the food and water?" Mary asked.

"Over the next hill," the child said, "we will find all that we need."

Joseph looked at his son. "Son, there is only desert here, there is no cactus, no oasis, nothing as far as I can see."

The boy smiled and seemed to go into a trance, placing his arms around his Mother's neck. "Over the next hill," he repeated.

Joseph started to speak and Mary held up her hand and shook her head, silencing her husband, but it was done in a loving manner. "We must believe our son," Mary said, the hint of a smile crossing her tired face, "for always when he has spoken, what seemed to be impossible became possible."

As the family slowly made their way across the desert slope, Jesus came out of his sleep-like trance. "Mother," Jesus said, "put me down, I will lead you where there is food—and water—enough to feed a multitude!" Mary did what her son bid her to do, and he ran ahead of the caravan, ahead of the guards who were there to protect them. "Let my son pass," Mary said in a loud voice, "For he will lead us to a place where our thirst will be quenched." Suddenly a voice in the wilderness seemed to whisper upon the winds, *And a small child shall lead them.*

I could see perfectly the way that Jesus ran, it was as if he had wings upon his feet—his golden hair had not yet turned to the reddish brown I was so familiar with—and just gazing upon him as a small boy filled me with a vast love too deep for words.

The boy ran up a small hill, and as he stood upon it, he spread his arms wide, and threw his head back, uttering words I could not understand. He then faced the caravan and his father and mother.

"Our cup shall never be empty," the boy said. "Come! Hurry!" With that he disappeared over the small hill and there, laid out upon the sands were pots filled with water and bowls that contained dates and nuts and herbs. There was bread and, yes, even wine. There was fish and small burning fires upon which to cook it. It was as if the heavens had opened up and placed the feast for a king before them. Indeed, it was a feast for a king—a king who was then but a boy. He was laughing with great joy as he dipped a wooden ladle in the water and took it to his mother, as the caravan descended upon the vast supper that was laid out for them.

Mary's eyes were wet with tears as Joseph helped her dismount from the donkey, and she knelt beside her son to take the wooden cup from his hands. She looked at the water as if it were something she had never seen.

"Drink, Mama," Jesus said.

Mary drank long and deep and then looked at her son. "How can this be?" she asked. People were walking around the bounty of food tentatively, carefully, as if they were seeing a phantom image that many see who have traveled too long through the desert lands.

The young boy, Jesus, wise beyond his years, smiled at his mother and said, "Ask of the Father what you will and, believing, it shall be done. When you said you were hungry and thirsty, I asked Him to help us—to please give to us what we need. Mother, why are you crying?"

"They are tears of joy, not sorrow, Jesus," she said. But I saw a sadness underneath the joy that led me to believe that she knew, long before he grew to manhood, what her son's fate would be. "These are tears of thankfulness," Mary added.

The entire throng stood around the circle of the feast, and unlike a hungry horde, they did not touch any of the food until the Holy Family gave their blessing to do so. Joseph hugged his son and said, "My boy, through you, this bounty has come to us, will you bless this food so that we may eat?"

Jesus raised his hands, and as he did, the throng knelt down, with their heads bowed.

"Heavenly Father," the boy said, "We give thanks for all that you have given to us. We give thanks for your showing us what is possible when we *believe*. May we never forget this day, even when the dark days come— for we know that what we ask shall be done. Thank you, Father. In joy and thankfulness, we pray. *Selah*."

There was so much food left over, that they could not load it all into the caravans after the feast was over. As this vision faded, that is when the memory of the wedding feast came back to me. For I remembered there was so much wine left over after the wedding feast, that there were not enough vessels to store it in. Suddenly I understood. I turned my face to the Master as the image of that long-ago journey faded from view.

"Do you understand, Mary?" He asked.

I pondered this question for a long while and could not venture an answer. And then the memory of a verse of the ancient scriptures came back to me.

"Be fruitful and multiply?" I asked.

He smiled that wondrous smile I had come to know so well.

"Yes," the Master said, "One of the first commandments that God gave in the beginning. That law did not mean just in the bearing of children. It was saying, whatever is lacking, ask and if you believe, and that which is most needed will manifest. But you must *believe*. When I was on the road back from Egypt, I called upon the Father, and He gave us what we needed."

I laughed—for I suddenly remembered the wedding feast—and what was it that was needed? The wine! And it was the Master's mother who had asked her son to do something about it!

Knowing my thoughts, the Master laughed too—and suddenly I re-lived that wonderful period where there was no sorrow, no worry, only the celebration of two souls who were coming together to share their lives as one.

I watched from this wonderful hillside the unfoldment of that scene on the day when the Master manifested the first of many miracles. When the wedding feast was held—the moon was high, the bride and groom were being carried on the shoulders of their respective families and we were all in a circle, dancing around them. There was much hilarity, people drank their fill of wine, and then drank some more. I would take part in the celebration, and then go to Mary to help in any way that I could. At that time, I had not seen the Master in many days. It was said that he had gone off into the wilderness for a "testing period," or a "cleansing period." I did not understand then, what the Master was doing. I know that his Mother anxiously watched from the doorstep for any sign of her eldest son (there were other children, but I shall write more of them later).

I had grown to be friends with this quiet, beautiful woman named Mary, the mother of the Master. And she welcomed me with the same love as her son welcomed me. She was a friend and a teacher to me. For now, let me return to this wonderful boisterous celebration. While outside in the garden there was the wedding party, in the kitchen was Mary, and Martha, myself, and Judy, a longtime friend of the family, and an early teacher of the Master. There was a problem in the kitchen. I could see from the friends gathered around Mary that they were consoling her over something I knew not of.

I made my presence known and said, "What is the trouble?"

"The trouble?" Martha said, almost mocking me. "The *trouble* is that the Mary has not seen her son in some forty days. Not even his closest followers know where he is, or if he is all right."

"It isn't that, Martha," Mary said, her voice filled a somber chord I had never heard. "It is true, I am anxious to know the whereabouts of my firstborn. But I know in my heart that he is safe. I have experienced too many things to not believe that. It would be a sin for me to worry about him—but still he is my son, and I am a mother. But the feast has just begun and the wine is running low. I do not know how this can be because I ordered enough for what seemed like an army!" Everyone laughed—even Mary herself—at this.

"No," she said, "something has happened. And I know not what. But I will—"

Suddenly a deep, male voice came out of the night—just outside the door of the house—and interrupted Mary.

"Have faith that all will be well!"

Many gasped in surprise as the Master, Jesus, came through the front door. Mary rose from her seat and her feet did not seem to touch ground as she leapt toward her son. She had bombarded him with questions.

"Jesus! Is it you?" Mary asked. "Is it really you? Where have you been? Why have been so long in coming? I've been so worried—What have you—?"

Jesus laughed, hugged her to his massive chest, interrupting her litany of questions. "Mother, dear sweet mother, give me a moment, will you please, to answer?"

"I am sorry," Mary said, regaining her composure. "It's just that I've had so much to do getting ready for this wedding, and I didn't know where you were. The only thing John told me was, 'He has gone to the wilderness, to pray.' Well, naturally, we all thought, you'd gone off to pray for a few hours, *not forty days!*" The motherly love, and the disapproval of his absence showed through, although she tried to keep her voice even.

The Master took his mother again in an embrace and sat down beside her. The women helping his blessed mother with the wedding feast took their leave, and let them have their privacy. I began to depart likewise, and the Master took my arm. "Mary, please don't leave. Stay with us. I want you to hear what I have to say."

Mary's eyes seem to roam around the room and then rest upon her son's face.

"Mother, I went to the desert for the Final Cleansing," the Master said. Mary's face darkened—but it was a fearful darkening. "Oh, my son!" She cried, "why didn't you tell me before you left?"

"Because you would have worried all the more," he said. "I had to do this alone—with only my closest ally at the time—Andrew." Andrew stood in the back of the crowd and wouldn't meet the gaze of Jesus or his mother. "It was the most difficult period of testing I have gone through so far, Mother," the Master said. Tears were flowing down Mary's face. Before she could ask another question, Jesus said, "I faced the Darkness—the Prince of Darkness—and he departed from me. And I feel made anew." The smile that came over his face lit up the entire room. "Dry your tears, Mother, all is well!" Mary looked upon her son—he was so strange to her in so many ways, in ways she could not yet comprehend.

And yet, above all else, he was her son. Called for a high purpose, yes—called to lead mankind out of the bondage of self—but it was easy to see that she, like the rest of us, didn't understand the full ministry of her son.

"All is well," Mary said, as she embraced her son again. "All is well for my eldest has come home. Please stay—there are so many here that are waiting to see and meet you."

Up to that point the wedding party was still going on, with Jesus and his friends carrying on unnoticed. Until someone broke into the kitchen from the party and said, "The wine is running low! We only have one pitcher left!"

Mary looked to her son. "Jesus, you know that I am the one who is hostess to this feast. We must do something—we cannot run out of wine!"

Jesus smiled upon his mother and tilted his head as if he didn't understand her question. It was obviously a joke between them.

"And Mother, what would you have me do? There are hundreds of guests here."

Mary, wiping away the tears, laughed and brushed the hair from the Master's face. "Did you think your mother would forget Egypt? How we were once starving and suddenly a banquet laid out for a king appeared out of nowhere? You told me—*your own mother*—to ask, and believing, it shall be done. Now what mother could forget that?"

Jesus threw his head back and laughed, put his arm around his mother and said, "Let us go into the feast. And exactly what is it you, the grand hostess of this marvelous feast, ask of me and the Father–Mother–God, to make this wedding complete?"

"A nice red wine," Mary said shyly, "with a bouquet they'll never forget—and a wonderful white with the taste and fragrance of spring!"

"As you have asked, dear Mother, it shall be done," the Master said.

When the bride and groom saw Jesus, they hurried through the wedding throng and they both ran into his open, massive arms.

"Blessed is this day," Jesus said, to all those gathered. "For God has brought these two souls together, and may all of their years be happy, may their children grow to be strong and healthy—and may the Spirit of Love—of God—forever dwell within their home! There is no tie more sacred than the marriage tie. The chain that binds two souls in love is made in heaven and man can never sever it in twain. Bless you both!" With that, a cheer went out from the crowd.

A man whose voice was heard but whose face could not be seen said, "Thank you, Jesus, for your blessing upon these two. Now where is the wine?"

Jesus laughed and said, "We have saved the best for last. Andrew, bring me those clay pitchers set in the corner, where the finest wine you shall ever taste is now held!"

"But, Master, those are only pitchers of water," Andrew said.

"Do you doubt me, Andrew?" Very quickly, almost comically, Andrew hurriedly brought the many pitchers to the table. There were no less than twenty large pitchers. "Help him, John!" Jesus commanded. The original spirit of celebration resumed. Mary, the mother of Jesus, stood anxiously beside Martha near the kitchen as all the pitchers were placed upon the table before the Master. I shall never forget this moment, even if I live to be eighty years old.

The Master placed his hands over the pitchers on the table and he blessed them in an ancient language—one that was unfamiliar to all those gathered. And then he said, "Pray what is wine? It is but water with the flavor of grapes. And what are grapes? They are but certain kinds of thought made manifest, and I can manifest that thought and water will be wine."

A hush fell over the crowd.

Jesus lowered his hands after a moment of silence and ordered one of the servants to give a pitcher to the ruler of the feast, who called in the bridegroom. "Hold out your cup, lad!" the man said. And behold, that which was once water poured into the chalice a deep reddish purple, and the crowd was amazed.

After the bridegroom had drank he said, "This is the best wine of all! You have reserved until the last." And everyone at the feast made their way to the table, laughing and joking and patting Jesus on the back and poured themselves the finest wine that was ever made. And Jesus rose and carried three mugs in his large hands—he handed one to his mother, one to me, and he kept one for himself.

Martha looked within her cup and was amazed and speechless. We laughed and Jesus said, "The wine is not for you to admire, Martha, drink. Drink!" And she did. We all did—and it was, like the wine of God, made manifest because of the request of a mother of her son. And I was witness and drank much that night. We all did. But unlike other wine, I was not left feeling heavy, nor did my head ache in the next morning light.

The ruler of the feast spread the word that Jesus, with a mighty thought, had stirred up the ethers till they reached the manifest, and, lo, the water blushed, and turned to wine.

Mary echoed the thought of the ruler, holding her glass up to her son. I also held my glass up to him and Mary said:

"Behold, the elements of the water recognized their Maker, they blushed, and became wine."

Jesus shook hands and embraced all in the wedding crowd, and I was a woman swept back into herself—watching this wondrous scene. I had seen many things, but never had I seen a man such as this—and though I was witness to many miracles (God grant that I may have time to write of them here), this was one of the happiest—for it took place at a celebration of love beginning, the lives of two becoming one—a wedding.

As my dream-vision ended, I can still see the Master's eyes looking into mine and even now I can feel his hand upon my shoulder. Much more I have yet to write, and it will not be easy—much of the rest of the Master's journey was hard—but this was one of the finest hours—one of the finest days I ever experienced. Even now, I can taste the wine, made from the fruit of God.

5

His Healing Touch

It is hard to believe at times . . . for me . . . so hard, when I
look back at who I once was, what I once did, to believe that
I was so blessed to have Jesus, the Master, as my beloved
companion—that he was not ashamed to ever be seen with
me, but that he welcomed me into his fold just as he welcomed the twelve men who traveled with him. There are
times when I struggle with the shadows of my past and, yes,
times when I am haunted by what I have done in the past—
but the most healing words that I ever did hear were, "Mary,
neither do I condemn thee." These words came from the *Son*
of God! Jesus was the voice of the Creator. I remember not a
circumstance or situation where he was shocked by the sins
of an individual. He embodied compassion, kindness, gentleness, and forgiveness. Above all else, when the Master said,
"Thy sins are forgiven thee. Move on with your life for you

are healed," the soul of the individual who had come for his aid, *was healed*. For the soul of the individual heard not only the voice of the Master, but in the Master's voice, they heard the very voice of God.

"God is love," the Master said many times, "and love is God. Where there are two who gather together in the name of love, God shall dwell in the midst of them." There is a secret, a mystery here—and all one must do is open the doors of the heart and believe. When the heart is open, the Master taught, and the mind is open to the possibilities, un-limited possibilities of what God can do, then Spirit pours forth through the individual, through the gathering, and the tangible, unmistakable feeling of the Source of all Love is present. I, even here, as I write these words in this dark place, I realize it is not a dark place at all, for He is the Light of the World, who came into the world, and dwells with us still.

For those who simply tried to believe, or desired to have communion with something greater than themselves, the Eternal Someone who has eternally been with us—but was unseen—was seen in the man Jesus. I heard many call him the Great Physician—for he had an education, an understanding of the body and the mind and the soul that others did not have. That, combined with the power he was imbued with from the heavens above, allowed miraculous healings to take place. And many times I watched him lay hands on the crippled, the halt, the palsied, the blind, the deaf, and the dumb, and upon the face of the Master was the most beautiful, brilliant smile the world has ever seen—I can see him even now with his eyes closed, his head thrown back, receiving the Holy Spirit to heal whatever ailed the person he was touching, and then I would watch the smile come upon the face of the sick person, and Jesus—with infinite kindness, compassion, and complete unconditional love would say, "All is well. Go in peace, for you are now made whole by the power of God." I, Mary of Magdalene, watched the crippled limbs straighten. I watched as the eyes of the blind, once film-covered to where you could discern no color in the eye except white, open wide and that which caused the blindness was gone in an instant. Many would cry out, praising God, the Master, and he would hold them as a mother holds a babe, as they wept with joy. And Jesus would turn his eyes to face us, the twelve Disciples and myself—and many others who followed him—and in that smile was, literally, the Light of the world—all of the joy and hope that you could possibly imagine was in that smile. To the person who was healed, after the Master touched them—be they young or old, rich or poor—they were made anew. Their despair, hopelessness, pain—it was gone from them—completely gone.

In my own life, there were many healings. I have written about the turbulent relationship with my father—and how I walked out and abandoned my family. I never saw my father alive again. He died within a year after our confrontation. I was haunted by the memory. I was haunted because there was no forgiveness, no closure, just the memory of our angry parting—and my mother standing there, tears streaming down her face, begging me not to go.

When I became friends with the Master I confessed what had happened with my father (even though I knew *he knew* all that I had ever done when he looked into my eyes), and I wept like a child as I told the story to Jesus. Like so many others who were in need of healing, the Master held me, too, and allowed me to cry freely.

"Mary," he said. "Do you not know that there is no separation between the world of the living, and the world of the Spirit? There is only a thin veil. When death comes, it is like a butterfly shedding its caterpillar shell. They pass on into the mansions of my Father's house, and abide in the home, or the place they have built for themselves. More than ever are they aware of the deeds they have done in the earth. They see and feel the deeds that were done out of love, and those that were committed out of selfishness. They come face to face with themselves, through the eyes of the people they have helped and those they have harmed."

I looked into his eyes and when I could find my voice I said, "So my father is still aware of me, and the things that he did to me and my mother?"

"Yes, Mary," the Master said. "For this reason, those who have passed through that veil to the Other World need the prayers, the forgiveness of those who are still in the earth."

I had believed, up until that time, that it was too late to forgive my father—because I thought he was no longer aware of me. Then Jesus spoke as if he were reading my thoughts.

"He needs you now more than ever," Jesus said. "For that which he did to you, he did out of ignorance. He has reviewed his life—every moment of it—every thought, every deed. Pray for him, Mary, that he may find the way to the Light, out of the land of shadows. For he regrets what he has done—and wishes more than anything that he had done things differently—that he had loved more. That is what the soul takes account of in the life hereafter: How much, or how little, did they show forth love to their fellow human beings. Is it not clear to see, in this light, what a heaven is built by many, and what a hell is created by others? God has not willed that any soul should perish, or be separate from Him, but people separate themselves from the Eternal Light of unconditional Love by their refusal to show forth love, by their refusal to forgive. These souls, Mary, dwell in the land of shadows, in places of regret and remorse. It is their own deeds, their own selfishness that leads them into these realms. They are not cast out and away from the love of God. For God never turns His love away from one of his children. But His children are blinded by their own selfishness."

I let the Master's words go deep into my heart. And for the first time, I felt sorry for my father. For he had been a stubborn man and, yes, sometimes cruel. In the light of what the Master had taught me, I felt sorry for him.

"Now," Jesus said, "Pray for him, that he may find his way to the lighted path that leads to the Throne of Grace, Mercy, and Light. He has much to learn, and much to unlearn. Close your eyes, and begin at the beginning, by letting go of all regret, all the anger. For, if your father knew what he was truly doing to you when he was upon the earth, he would not have done it. He didn't know any better, Mary. Set him free."

I felt the hands of the Master gently upon my head and in an instant I saw my father. He was in a gray place—a place of shadows—just as the Master said. He was surrounded by other souls who were just like him! Those who had been harsh and narrow-minded, some had been violent. It was a place not on this earth, but it was near to the earth. I could see my father was chained by all that was his own doing. My friends, this image was as clear as if I were physically in a real place. Quickly my father seemed to look through me, and then at me. Because of the Master's touch, I felt nothing but love for this poor soul—for I knew he did not know the consequences of his actions. I understood that what is done in physical life must be reaped in the life hereafter. The words of the Master came back to me, "That which you sow, is that you will one day reap. In this life, or in the next." I felt pity for my father, and I prayed for him. I could see him weeping in a corner of this dark and gloomy place, and others were mocking his tears and his remorse. "Help me," he said—to me—to God—to anyone who would listen. I knew in my heart this was the first time he had ever asked for help. His pride, in life, had held him back from ever asking for help. Now, his heart was changed.

"Please, help me," he said again, wailing. I could still feel the Master's hands upon my head, but I could also see that I was illuminated in this dark, foreboding place.

"Father, I forgive you," I said aloud. Upon hearing the sound of my voice, it was as if he was seeing me for the first time. "Oh, Mary, sweet Mary, I am so sorry for what I did to you. I am surrounded by remorse and oh! The regrets, I so wish I could undo so much of what I have done. I am undone." He wept tears anew and I could feel his anguish and his pain and I felt nothing but compassion for him—for he was so lost.

"Tell him to look upward, Mary," Jesus said, "toward the Light—the Light of Eternal Love. There are Guardians that will take him to the Light."

When Jesus spoke, it was as if the heavens opened up and a great shaft of brilliant light filled the dark quarters where my father lay. Others who surrounded him shrieked and ran from the light. They tried to tell my father not to look at the light, that it would burn him, or hurt him.

"Father," I said, "Look up, look up! There is a Light, an all-loving Light coming for you." My father looked confused but when he looked up, all at once his countenance changed—I could see, for the first time, hope in his eyes."

"Mary, is it real?" My father asked, his voice filled with wonderment.

"Yes, Father," I said, "The Light of unconditional love. Follow it. You needn't stay there any longer. You are free. Pray, father, pray that the Light take you out of that place of darkness and shadow."

My father's voice faltered. "But Mary, I am not worthy . . . of this . . . wondrous gift." His voice was breaking. I felt Jesus' hands, so warm upon my head, I don't know how I knew what to say, except that the Master's spirit was guiding me.

"Father, all are worthy," I said. "I forgive you. I love you, and that is all that exists for you now—love—eternal. Go now, to the Light—there are angels and guides to help you."

The Light shone down brilliantly upon my father, and his shadowy complexion—his face that appeared so gray and old was now youthful and was filled with light. I saw a great angel descend from the Light, with her arm outstretched.

"Come, Marcus," the angel said, in a voice filled with infinite love, "It is time to go home." My father tentatively lifted his hand, and looked at me, all the while his lips moved, quietly saying prayers of thanksgiving. "I love you, Mary. I—I have so much I want to say to you—but—"

"Go now, Father," I said. "There will be time—an eternity of time for us to talk." After speaking those words, I watched as he wept tears of joy and relief. "Oh, Mary!" I heard him say, as he ascended up into the Light, taking the hand of the angel. The last words I heard him say were, "Thank you, God. Thank you." The Light closed up into the heavens, and I heard the voice of Jesus saying, as if from a long distance away, "Come back now, Mary, come back. All is well—your father will be taken care of."

I opened my eyes and saw the Master's face, so close to mine. I wrapped my arms around his neck, my voice choked with tears—not of sadness, but happiness, I could say not a word. The Master just held me. "Bless you, Mary, for what the Father has ordained for you to see," he said. "Now you know that no soul is ever truly lost. All that is required of a soul who finds itself in the shadowlands is to ask for God's help. Despair, hopelessness, regret, these are as demons that possess so many souls—in this world and in the next. If they would but just ask for Divine aid, God will send His angels to them to help carry them to the realms of love.

"But," he added, "the soul must ask for help of itself. You know full well that one cannot help another soul who does not want nor desire your help. So pray, pray often for those who have passed beyond the veil to the next world. Many think they are lost. Because they think and believe this, it is so. Likewise, if they believe there is redeeming grace, that there is forgiveness, that there is Light, then, too, it will be so. What a man or woman thinks in their heart, so it is."

I felt the truth of the Master's words and never again in my own life did I ever despair after that day. If I felt myself slipping into negative thoughts, or felt discouraged, I would pray and ask to be delivered from such thoughts, and, as the Master said—it was so. I was healed. I never dreamed, though, that when a loved one passes from this world at physical death—going "beyond the veil," as the Master put it, that there still can be communion with them—that there can be a healing.

In my own life, three great healings took place with the Master. I was saved from the religious zealots who were going to stone me to death. The Master released me from the seven devils. The turbulent relationship I had with my father was healed—because of the Master's mystic vision. I have learned that it's never too late—no, never too late to forgive and be forgiven.

Many other healings I saw the Master do in his walk through the earth. The Great Physician (as the Master was called by many) used many different methods to heal the masses that came to him.

For some individuals, he would simply say *the Word*, it was a powerful word that restored wholeness to a person who was ill. On one occasion, I watched in awe when the Master healed a blind man. The Master leaned down and gathered together earth from a field. He formed the earth into a poultice and placed two packs over the blind man's eyes.

"Leave these packs upon your eyes for a day," Jesus said. "And tomorrow, when you remove them, you shall see." The following day I was traveling with the Disciples and the Master to Bethsaida. The man came running down the road calling after the Master—tears of joy spilled down his cheeks.

"I can see! Praise God, I can see!" he exclaimed to Jesus, and fell at his feet. Jesus lifted him gently from the ground and gave him a blessing.

"Your faith has made you whole," Jesus said. "Bless you."

"No," said the man, holding tightly onto the Master, "it was you who healed me!"

Jesus smiled upon the man. "I of myself can do nothing," the Master said. "But it is the Father–Mother–God who works in and through me that makes manifest these wondrous works."

The man looked deeply into Jesus' eyes and all at once, in a quiet but powerful voice he said, as he again fell to his knees, "You are the One who has been promised. You are the Christ—the living God made flesh."

Jesus leaned down to the man and whispered into his ear, "I am He. Go your way now and tell no man what has been revealed to you. For my time has not yet come."

I did not understand what Jesus meant then, but I do now. He was the Christ, the Anointed One, the promised Messiah—but before that day, no one had identified the Master as such in public. When Jesus said, "My time has not yet come," I realize now that should word have spread throughout the countryside of this truth, that Jesus was who he truly was—the Christ—then, those who despised him, those who called him a sorcerer and a black magician, would have come after him and he would not have been able to carry on with his work of spreading the Word: That God dwells within the heart of every individual.

The man promised Jesus that he would not utter a word. But when he returned to his people with his sight restored, people asked him how it was possible that he could see when he was blind since birth.

"A strange and beautiful man came to me," the man said, "and placed packs upon my eyes, and my sight was restored." It was not long before word spread to the Romans and to the High Priests that Jesus had healed the man. But the man withheld what he had promised not to tell: That Jesus was the Christ.

Even in his greatness, Jesus remained humble. He always said, "It is the God who works through me, the instrument of my body and mind that brings the healing to pass. All people have the ability to do this if they would but attune their hearts, minds, and souls to the Infinite God. After I am gone, there will be many others who will come in my name, and there shall be healings—the lame shall walk, the deaf shall hear, the blind shall receive their sight."

I, Mary of Magdalene, bore witness to these things. And I keep the experiences close to my heart and I am made warm by the memory.

The Master taught the multitudes many things concerning healing. A dear friend of mine, Levi, a carpenter who had worked with Jesus in his youth, remembered that Jesus had said the body was like a harp, and when its strings were too relaxed, or too tense, the instrument was out of tune, and then sickness came. When the harp of man is out of tune, the vast expanse of nature may be searched for remedy. There is a cure for every ailment of the flesh. Jesus told me that the will of man is supreme—and by the vigorous exercise of will, man may make tense a chord that is relaxed, or may relax one that is too tense, and thus may heal himself, by the power of God.

"When man has reached the place where he has faith in God, in nature and himself," the Master said, "he knows the Word of power—his word is balm for every wound, is cure for all of the ills of life. A thousand things produce disharmony and make men sick—a thousand things may tune the harp, and make people well.

"The healer is the man who can inspire faith. The tongue may speak to human ears, but souls are reached by souls that speak to souls."

That is what the Master Jesus did: His soul spoke to the souls of the weak and the weary and the downtrodden. And whether he lay his hands upon them, or spoke the Sacred Word, as he did for my brother Lazarus, and called him back to life—whatever the method the Master used, the Source of the healing was the same: God.

"The virtue from the hand or breath may heal a thousand more," Jesus said. "But Love is the ultimate healer. Many of the broken chords in life, and discords that so vex the soul, are caused by evil spirits of the air, or evil thoughts, that men cannot see. These lead men on through ignorance to break the laws of nature and of God. These powers act like demons, and they rend the man. They drive him to despair. But he who is a healer, true, is master of the soul, and can, by force of will, control these evil ones and drive them away. But the human vessel alone cannot perform the healing. But humankind has helpers in the higher realms that may be called upon and they will help to drive out the demons, or the dis-ease, and then healing will come by natural result."

Again and again, the Master taught that God dwells within each and every one soul.

"The time has come," the Master said, "when God will be worshipped not in the temple or any building, but in the secret place of the inner heart. *That* is the temple, my friends. For God is not within Jerusalem, nor in the holy mount outside of your own selves, but lo, He is in every heart. God is Spirit. Those who worship him must worship him in spirit—from within—and without—by being true. Being true—meaning well for others. This is the first step that will bring God closer to your awareness and your heart—try to love others as God loves you. The more you love one another, the more you will feel the eternal love of your Maker. He's right here! In your midst, but you ask, 'where is God? Where is he? I want to see and hear him.' Each and every soul is like a flower floating down a great river. The great river is God. The path of the river winds here and there, always moving, though. The flowers float across the top—in complete freedom—in harmony with the flow—The flow of the river of God. I have come to remind you that you are always in the river of God—you cannot be away from God because *all that is, is God!*"

When the Master said those words, I looked skyward and there was a dove gently descending. And those who were listening with me—my sister, my brother Lazarus, and of course all of the men he traveled with, saw the dove descend and land upon his shoulder. She was a mourning dove and nestled her head in the fall of his hair, just beneath his ear. The Master turned his face and lifted his shoulder that he could feel the bird all the more tenderly.

"Look at her," the Master said. "Does she worry about where her food will come from? Does she worry about not having enough twigs to build her home-nest?" The dove fluttered its wings and settled upon the Master's shoulder as a mother bird would settle upon its eggs—tilting her head this way and that—cooing and cooing.

"She does not worry nor have a care because she lives in the living ether of air and sky—and she knows where to find all her food, all of her nesting needs, because the Living Creator *tells her* where to go—and she listens." He picked up the bird in one of his powerful hands. I can see the strong veins running across the back of his hand and up his forearm—the bird was nearly dwarfed in his powerful, but loving grasp. He held her up for all to see.

"If God looks after and loves this little mother-bird, imagine how much more he cares for you—a thinking, self-aware creature—capable of being a great channel for help and healing to the masses!" He lifted his hand and the bird took off, spiraling upwards in a divine flight.

"The birds of the air know their Maker, but mankind, in his short-sightedness, worries and fears over this and that." The Master's face was filled with compassion and sadness both. It was like a passing shadow upon his face and then he looked at the crowd and smiled again. And the crowd, responding to his emotions, *felt the sadness* that indeed, we had forgotten and lost our faith. But then, when he smiled, the winds uplifted the emotions of all those gathered and he said, "And that is why I have come to you, to earth. To bring to your remembrance what your soul already knows, but your small mind has forgotten. I have come to show you this—and more."

A palsied man, shaking violently stood up and walked toward the Master. Tears running down his face. "Master," he said, "I want to remember what my soul already knows. Help me clear the blocks I have placed in my mind that made me forget. I—I want to remember and *live. Can you help me live better?"* The Master received the man in a full embrace—his powerful arms surrounding the little, crippled man, who could not stand straight nor stop shaking. The Master embraced the man like the mother–bird enfolds her chicks. And then, a sigh, in complete relief and unison arose from the crowd when Jesus opened his arms.

The man was no longer bent and crippled and twisted. He stood firm and solid. The shaking was gone. His body was perfect.

"Master," the man cried, "I—I am healed! I am whole again." Tears arose in the Master's eyes as he gazed upon the man.

"Go, now, my friend, and do what I have done," the Master said. Embracing the man again. "As you are set free from your limited self, go and help others become free—in the name of the all–loving God."

"I will," the man said. "I will," wiping tears from his face. "You are the One who was promised from ages past, aren't you? You are . . . Christ." Jesus smiled at the man and looked heavenward. Again, he said, "I of myself can do nothing, but I will that the Christ—the living perfect essence of Love in activity, fill my heart, mind, and body. And, as it was promised, my mind, body, heart, and soul are at one with the Father–Mother–God. I am *he.* I am the image of each one of you—in the future. What I do, you shall do also. Greater things than these shall you do." He looked again upon the man who was healed. "Go now, friend, and heal others, in my name—in the name of Love—in the name of the Almighty God."

The crowd then opened, and the sick and lame and crippled came forth, and Jesus, the living Christ, laid his hands upon them all and no matter how badly they were crippled, or hurt, they were made whole. It was love, my friends, complete love that healed them all. And every time a person was healed, he said, "Go and do likewise for others. Give them hope. Love them—all—as your Creator loves each of you."

I then brought the Master a cup of water in a stone jar, for he had talked long hours and was tired. He took the water from my hand and said, "Those of you who give a stranger a cup of water in my name, give a cup of water to God." Then he drank. And I wept.

"Lady Magdalene," he said, "You are a beautiful creature, made in the image of the Creator. Thank you for the water." And I went away for there were more people who needed healing—and though my heart wanted to stay in his presence day and night, I knew I had to leave him and let him do his work. And I had work to do as well.

It is long after dark and the lamp-oil is almost empty and so is my quill and precious ink—brought to me by a man whose name I do not know. I know and have faith that in the morning, I will awaken and find the well filled again, and more parchment on which to write. Good-night, my beloved Master. Good night Jesus. I hope you visit me in my dreams.

6

Conversations with Jesus
on the Kingdom

I have been writing for days upon days—and I know not what day this is. The readers (if there be any—and I pray there will) may be discouraged or disappointed when they see that these diary pages are not dated. I can only tell you this: It has been some three years since the Master was put to death upon the cross, and then rose again upon the third day and walked and talked with people of all climes, all walks of life. That I must write at a later time, for now I must tell you the mystery, the secret that lives within the heart of every human being: The mystery of the Kingdom of God. So many people, even the Master's closest followers misinterpreted the meaning of the Kingdom. Although the Master said, "The Kingdom of God, of heaven is within you," it was beyond the comprehension of the masses. He taught his followers, and those who would listen—and there were thousands upon thousands who would hang upon his every word—that each person has within them the "Divine Spark of the Creator." The Master was called a blasphemer because he said, "Ye are gods becoming." The Pharisees misinterpreted this also—and sought to lay hands upon him and kill the Master for uttering such words. Yet his words were true.

That we live and breathe and are self-aware—the Master taught—is evidence that the Great Creator is cognizant of every soul. Because God is the source of all life, no soul could exist if there was not an unseen bond between the soul and its Maker.

"It is God who gives you life," the Master said. "The very essence of the beating of your heart is God playing upon the strings of that heart. The Kingdom is not far off, neither is it hidden from you. But it is in a secret place—the Secret Place of the Most High."

The Master was speaking on a vast hillside on that day and the throngs surrounded him, but not a sound could be heard when he spoke. All were as little children, listening to the living words of life, of God. All at once a small boy came running through the crowds and came up to Jesus. The Master paused and looked down at the boy and smiled. Peter and the other Disciples moved toward Jesus to shoo the boy away, but Jesus lifted his hand and stopped them.

"Welcome, my little one," the Master said, "Come and sit with me." The boy was overjoyed as the Master knelt down and the child climbed into Jesus' lap. He stroked the boy's hair and held him with great tenderness. The boy was enthralled with Jesus.

"I say to you all," the Master said, "that unless you become—in heart and spirit—as this small child, you will not see the Kingdom of God. This child worries not where his next meal is coming from, nor does he worry for tomorrow. He is happy in the moment—innocent and wide-eyed at the marvels of the day. Each day for him holds adventures and experiences that he welcomes. He is himself and knows not how to be anything but his own happy self. He is at one with all that is around him, emanating the light of pure love."

The little boy chuckled and toyed with the Master's hair. Other children then came up to the Master and he blessed each and every one of them, laying his hands upon some, uttering kind words to others. That was when I saw in the Master's eyes a child-like quality. He was happy with the delightfulness of the children around him. My heart was filled with gladness for I knew that as the Master felt such delight and happiness, so did the throngs surrounding him. Except for his detractors, the Pharisees and the Sadducees, who were jealous of the Master's hold upon the crowd.

"What about the kingdom of Rome?" one of the Pharisees asked. "How can we possibly find heaven when the Romans tax us to no end, and rule with such iron fists, without mercy? When will that come to an end and the kingdom of which you speak come into being here on earth?" Jesus looked upon the man, who was standing next to Judas ben Iscariot. Judas was one of the twelve who I never trusted—for he was a political zealot, seized with the idea that the Master had come to the earth to overthrow Rome.

"Render unto Caesar that which is Caesar's," the Master said, "and render unto God that which is God's. The Kingdom of Heaven, of God, is within you. You need only ask, and you shall receive in abundance if you would but believe that there is a greater power than yourself who guides your life. Take note and thought of your inner life, take time apart from the outer cares of the world, and enter within your temple—the temple of God within your heart and mind. And there, and only there, will you find peace."

Judas and the man who asked the question looked disappointed, for they believed Jesus to be the One who had been promised to be sent—the Messiah—but they believed that he had come to establish a new government, a new kingdom upon the earth. Fools. The Master had taught all along that when enough people sought God through the temples of their own hearts, then there would be a change in the outer world. I felt in my heart a shudder and a sense of foreboding—I feared for the Master for some reason—and I cannot tell why or what that fear was—other than there was something that had to do with Judas, and those zealots who wanted to proclaim the Master as a king, as the master of a new movement in the land. I knew that the Master's coming was a revolution of the heart. Jesus had come into our midst to break down the barriers that the mind had imposed—and sought to show mankind what was possible when the mind was made one with the Great

Mind, the mind of God.

Little did I know at the time how far Judas would go to try to force Jesus to show the hypocritical leaders of the church and of the Romans, who He truly was. But Judas misunderstood. So many times he had seen the Master vanish, as if into thin air when his enemies sought to lay hands upon him. I do believe that if it had been the Master's purpose, he could have overthrown Rome in a moment with the wave of his hand—but that was not his purpose. He came to tell us that love was the only force, the only power that could turn the tide of darkness and tyranny.

As I looked at Jesus, I could feel that he was instilling into the hearts and minds of all the people around him that which was truth—without saying a word. I watched as the crowd seemed to become aware and awake. It was as if they were seeing truth for the very first time.

At that point, a former Roman guard—who was present when my brother, Lazarus, was brought forth from the grave, and was converted and changed when he saw my brother come forth alive and healthy and well—again questioned the Master.

"Master," he said, "I was there when Lazarus came forth by the very power of your words. I know that we are eternal. My motto was, before then, as we Romans say, *Carpe diem*, or as others have it, 'Eat, drink, and be merry, for tomorrow we die.' But now I know we should live not so much for this life here on earth, as for the life to come, in heaven. And therefore, Master, teach us somewhat of that life—for in that life, I suppose, we shall find the Kingdom which you proclaim."

The Master smiled, remembering the Roman, who had disguised himself so that his fellow soldiers would not recognize him. For it was ordered in that day that the Romans were to watch over Jesus, and spy upon him, but should any of them become a follower, it would mean death.

"My brother, your heaven is not far away, and it is not a place of metes and bounds, not a country to be reached—it is a state of mind. God never made a heaven for man. He never made a hell. We are creators and we make our own. Now, cease to seek for heaven in the sky—just open up the windows of your hearts, and, like a flood of light, a heaven will come and bring a boundless joy. Then the work-a-day world will not be hard, nor cruel.

"No, my friend," the Master said, "you will not have to wait for that life to behold the Kingdom. For as I have spoken, the Kingdom of Heaven is within you, here and now, and, just as you open your eyes in the morning and behold the light of the sun, so you only need open the eyes of your soul to behold the Kingdom of Heaven in all its glory."

The Master went on to unfold his teaching of the spiritual kingdom that he said he came to manifest—and show mankind what was possible. He said that all our earthly philosophies are either wrong or miss the one thing needful—the faith that God, the Maker of all things, is not something distinct and separate and far removed from our eyes, but that God is bound up in us, and we in him, the noble and the slave, the good and the evil—all brothers and sisters—sons of the eternal Father-Mother-God.

"Whether you are rich or poor," the Master said, "whether you are a priest or a peasant—all are equal in the eyes of the all-loving, all-forgiving Creator. If you choose love instead of hate, cherish instead of despise, aid instead of contend with your fellow man, then all our transitory troubles will pass away, and infinite happiness and eternal peace will come to you."

The little boy still sat in Jesus lap, looking into his eyes and smiling and laughing. The Master hugged the little boy.

"The Kingdom of Heaven has been concealed from the wise and revealed unto babes," the Master said. "Relinquish all that is cynical, and see in your brother—yea, even him who would despise you, look for the spark of the Creator in the eyes of all people you shall meet. And as you seek it, you shall find it. For it is not a thing afar off—it is within your own heart.

"The Kingdom of Heaven is the place where your awareness is married, blissfully, with the One who created you. All of you are His children, and as all parents seek to have closeness with their children, so does your Father in Heaven seek to be close with you. This kingdom is no great mystery—but in its simplicity it is hidden from the logical mind. Each day, as the dawn arises, pray to the All-loving God facing East, and feel the peace that comes into your soul. Silence yourselves each day and ask that you be filled and made aware of God's Divine Spirit. Let not the outside world, and all of its illusions distract you from this important task. Those who would find God must worship Him in Spirit. Within the silence of yourselves, you shall find the Kingdom—and peace that passes all understanding shall be yours. I am come among you to show you God manifest in the flesh. And the words that I speak, I speak not of myself, but I speak the words that the Creator has given me to speak.

"Within the silence of yourselves, pray in earnest. Do not sacrifice birds and animals, for these are of the very Kingdom of Heaven itself. God does not require blood sacrifice—He only desires that we love one another, and love Him, above all else. And this is a promise: When you seek to commune with the Most High from within your own selves, you shall see the Kingdom—and all that has been hidden shall be revealed unto you. For God has known and loved you since before the foundations of the world—and He shall bring to your remembrance all things—whatsoever I have told you. Again, I speak not of myself, but that you may know the truth, even as it has been given to me from the beloved Creator who has sent me. You have witnessed that the lame have walked, the blind have seen, the deaf have heard. All diseases have been healed by the touch of my hand—but I of myself can do nothing—it is the Father-Mother-God working in me and through me that manifests these miraculous works. Hence, go forth and be humble, for you too shall manifest these gifts. You shall be given the power to heal, to cast out demons, to break the shackles that bind your mind and soul—if you would but seek God where He may be found—within your own heart."

"Master," a voice cried from the crowd, "teach us to pray that we may commune with this God of whom you speak."

Jesus bowed his head for a moment and then he looked upward into the heavens and said, "Bow your heads. And with sincerity and earnestness pray in this manner:

"Our Father, Our God who art in Heaven and in earth,
Hallowed and sacred is thy name!
Give us this day, our daily bread, the needs of the body.
Forgive us our debts and our sins, to the degree that we
Forgive those who sin against us.
Lead us not into the temptations of the world

But deliver us from all evil and temptations from the world.
Open our eyes to thy Holy Kingdom now
And fill our hearts with peace.
For Thine is the kingdom, the sacred power,
And the eternal Glory, forever and ever.
As we believe it is so, so it is. Selah."

Others sought to know more of the Kingdom of Heaven and Jesus taught a parable. He said a certain man possessed a field, and the soil was hard and difficult to plow. By constant toil he scarcely could provide enough of food to keep his family from hunger. One day a miner who could see beneath the hard ground, in passing on his way, saw this poor man and his unfruitful field. He called the weary toiler and he said, "My brother, know you not that just below the surface of your barren field rich treasures lie concealed? You plow and sow and reap in a scanty way, and day by day you tread upon a mine of gold and precious stones. This wealth lies not upon the surface of the ground, but if you will but dig away the rocky soil, and go down deep into the earth, you need no longer till the soil for nothing.

The man believed. "This miner surely knows," he said, "and I will find the treasures hidden in my field." He dug away the rocky soil, and deep down in the earth he found a mine of gold.

Jesus then said, "The sons of men are toiling hard upon the desert plain, and burning sands and rocky soils—are doing what their fathers did, not thinking there is any other way. But then a Master comes, and tells them of a hidden wealth, that underneath the rocky soil of earthly things are treasures that no man can imagine or fathom.

"In the heart of all people the richest gems abound," the Master said. "He who wills may open up the door and find them all. Open the doors of your hearts, my beloved, and your mind, for there you will find your soul, your treasure, and you shall find communion with God—and toil will no longer be a burden. Beneath the surface of your outer selves, God lives, and longs to give you the treasure of harmony, peace, love, and tranquility. These are the things you long for—such are the Kingdom of God, of Heaven."

With this the Master then received all the sick and the lame, and spoke the Sacred Word and hundreds, if not thousands were healed. And I saw above me, on another hillside the so-called high priests, the hypocrites, and I knew in my heart they were conspiring against the Master. I saw Judas walking away from the other Disciples and counseling with one of those who despised Jesus.

Again, I felt coldness and fear in my heart, but I tried to do as the Master said, to pray for the enemy. I did not know why then, but I perceived Judas to be the enemy, although in his heart I believe he thought he was doing the right thing.

He would eventually be the one who would conspire against the Master and turn him over to the High Priests. It is something I cannot bear to speak of now, but I will in the days to come.

Now, it is almost dawn and I long to see the sun through the small window and commune from within with the Master. It is true, what he spoke: The Kingdom of Heaven is not afar off—but one must silence the voice of the mundane self in order to see it—and to see Him. Many times He has come to me in the Silence of myself. And now, weariness fills me and I long to have His strength give me the ability to carry on, and tell the remainder of the story of when God came to earth as a man, and set us all free.

7

The Final Days and Hours

Word had spread far and wide among the Romans as well as the many religious sects that Jesus was proclaiming himself to be a "king." Nothing could be further from the truth— but the crowds, his followers, wanted him to be king—one that would overthrow the tyranny of Rome. In his gentleness, a great tempest had arisen. In his compassion for all mankind, his enemies came out of the woodwork. When he brought solace, healing, and relief to souls who had none on the Sabbath, he was called a sorcerer.

So when he said, "My brothers and sisters I must go to Jerusalem," I felt a cold wind of dread blow through me. For in Jerusalem were his greatest enemies—the ones who feared the Master would overthrow the old established kingdoms and churches, and establish his reign—his kingdom—upon the earth, in the sacred places of Jerusalem. If only they had listened closely to his stories, parables they would have realized that the Master spoke of the Kingdom as a place of the heart—where mankind could meet God face to face.

I had no rational reason to fear—but my soul knew what was coming, my rational mind did not. For I had seen Jesus evade his persecutors. I had seen him vaporize—disappear—right before the eyes of the spies of Pilate, and the high priest Caphias. The latter was violent and ruthless. It was said that he would behead or crucify even one of his own army for an idle criticism.

In my restlessness in times past, I sought the refuge of Mary, the Master's mother for solace and guidance. If anyone knew the outcome of all that would come to pass, she would.

I was shocked when I went to her summer home near Gennesaret. Her face was care-worn—it was as if she had aged overnight some twenty years. When she opened the door I immediately went to her waiting arms.

"Mary!" I said, "are you ill with a fever? What—"

She interrupted me with a smile and a wave of the hand.

"My child, I am fine," Mary said. "There is a strange wind blowing through the places where my son has visited—and his enemies are closer than I anticipated." She sat down but never let go of my hand. I saw tears in her eyes. She turned her face from me that I would not see them. Then she said, "He is my son, Mary, but he is not my son. I know who he is—and it was prophesied eons ago that the Son of Man, the Son of God would come and he would be persecuted, and die in the tempest of ignorance by the unruly mob. In my heart I have pondered this since I conceived him. Since the visitation of Archangel Gabriel, I knew that this man who would be born of me would be a sacrifice for the many. Now his time has come—I can feel it in my heart.

I was overwhelmed by what Mary said. And in my heart I wanted to deny that any harm would come to the Master.

"The prophets have written much, Mary," I said. "If what they have written was true, then God will take care of your son. I, too, have been uneasy and afraid. I am amazed and awed by what I have seen. Your son has manifested love in a way that no teacher has ever been able to show forth on the earth. He embodies that Divine Father-Mother-God, the Christ, and so I don't know why I am afraid for him." I paused in my words for I felt a lump in my throat and I did not want to break down in the presence of the Master's mother. I wanted to be strong because I could see that her own heart was breaking.

Mary took my other hand and placed it over her heart. "It is because you love Jesus," Mary said. "You above all other women, my son has loved and loves you. You are one of his Disciples. That is why you feel the things you do. It is the human side of us that fears for what we cannot foresee. Even though we have seen him raise the dead, heal the sick, and manifest miracles beyond anything the world has ever seen, he is a still a man. I know you love him, Mary—and it may lend you little comfort to say, 'Do not be afraid.' But I say this because my son hears voices beyond our hearing—he communes with the Unseen God face-to-face. So wherever he goes, he goes not alone. That is what keeps me going on: for Jesus is his own person, but he is also God incarnate." Mary paused a moment and shook her head in bewilderment—and smiled. "That he came from my own womb still fills me with awe," she said, and then her countenance became serious. "In my heart I know that should the worst happen—should my son die at the hands of his enemies, his voice shall not be silenced. For he has spent these past three years proclaiming the Divine heritage—that God dwells within the heart of every man, every woman. And should this be his fate—should he be taken by those of the darkness, I know that God will be with him and take care of him.

"We must have faith, Mary," she added. "Look at you. You once walked with the kings and princes and were sought after by royalty and wore the finest gowns from Persia. I have witnessed the change in you, and it is nothing short of a miracle. Be strong, my child, for you too are a walking testament to the legacy of my son: No matter how far one may stray into the world, God is always present with us, and within us. You, of all people, know this."

Indeed I did. I was filled with awe and wonder at the changes in me. As I said in the beginning of these writings, there was a time when I was divorced from my own soul, a material thing that was be used for the pleasure and satisfaction of other men and myself. I actually smiled at the memory of who I once was. For had I not traveled that road of darkness, I never would have found the light embodied in Jesus, the Christ.

"Mary," I said, "I do not regret one step in my life, even when it took me into the darkest regions of the world's most sensuous experiences. For though it was a dark road that I trod, that road led me to your son, the Master. There are no mistakes or missteps. All roads lead back to God. That is what your son has taught me. I am not holy, nor am I less human. Your son awakened my soul to its true heritage and brought it to the forefront of my mind. Such a priceless gift he has given me." I looked deep into the eyes of Jesus' mother. "You are blessed, Mary, above all women—for through you came the Light of the world."

In that moment all the fears and dread we had felt were completely gone. God had come into our midst and calmed the turbulent seas of our emotions and whispered, "All is well."

Mary and I looked at one another and together we said, in unison, "All is well."

We both laughed aloud—and clung to each other—and though there were tears, they were tears of joy, for we felt the calming, peaceful state of God in our midst. Such is what Jesus had taught us: "Where two or more are gathered, there is God—there am I, in the midst."

For the rest of the afternoon, I told her stories of the marvels I had seen Jesus perform. I told her of a day where the crowds were pressing upon Jesus as he was trying to board Peter's boat. Hordes of people were clamoring to have Jesus heal them—and he had been healing the masses all day, and it was now eventide. I could see the exhaustion in the Master's eyes and he longed only to lay his head upon the bed and rest. Still the crowd pressed and pressed upon him and all at once the Master said, "Who touched me?"

It was Peter who looked at the Master as if he had gone mad. "Who touched you?" Peter asked with such incredulity it was amusing. "Hundreds, yea, thousands are pulling and pushing to be near you and yet you say, 'Who touched me?'

"No," Jesus said. "I felt the Power go out from me to someone in need. Someone who has great faith and who needed . . . God."

Peter tried to keep pulling Jesus to the boat and Jesus stopped in the middle of the boisterous crowd. With a loud voice Jesus cried, "Stop! Everyone move back—NOW!" And then, it was like the parting of the

Red Sea in the days of Moses. Immediately the crowd fell back and pressed upon the Master no longer. Suddenly, it was just the twelve Disciples and myself standing some short distance from the boat. There was not a sound to be heard but the small waves crashing upon the beach. All the people were seated, bewildered to find themselves sitting when a moment before, they were seeking to be near the Master. Their heads were bowed.

"Who touched me?" Jesus asked, with a voice of infinite kindness and compassion, but with great power.

A woman, whose name I found out later was Ulai, came up to Jesus and fell before his feet. Tears were streaming down her face.

"It was I, Master," Ulai said.

"Stand up, my child," Jesus said. "And tell me what happened.

"It is all right. We are all friends here." He reached out and touched her shoulder and immediately she began to speak.

"I have been afflicted with an illness of the blood," she said. "In my womanly parts I have been filled with great pain and the bleeding has been constant and I cannot go out into public because of it. The doctors cannot help me, they have said that I may die."

She began to cry and Jesus held her close, encouraging her to go on with her story.

"I knew you would be passing this way," she said. "And I thought, 'If I could just touch the hem of his garment, I would be healed.' I am sorry, Master, but I ran through the crowd and I fell to the ground and touched the hem of your robe. And immediately, I could feel a great heat and I knew I was healed."

All the people surrounding us marveled at the woman's story.

Jesus smiled upon Ulai. "Never in all of this land have I seen such faith, and that faith has made you whole, my child. There is no need for you to be sorry. You have demonstrated what I have been trying to teach to so many." He addressed the crowd. "By the power of thought, belief, and desire, all things are possible—if you would only believe. For God resides within you as He does within me. And as this woman has shown you, her faith, which she thought was in me, but was truly of God, has made her whole. Blessed art thou, my dear one."

She knelt and kissed the Master's feet. "I know you are the One who has been promised to come. I know you are the Christ." She whispered the last part so the crowd would not hear.

"My child," the Master said, "What God has revealed to your heart and your soul is true, but tell no man. For my time is not yet come. You are blessed and shall be a great channel of healing to others in your life. Go now, and spread the good news of your healing, but keep secret that I Am." When the Master said the words "I Am" it was as if the very ground itself shook with the power of his words. Again, I knew I was in the presence of a beautiful creature called man, and I was also in the presence of the all-loving, all-compassionate Creator of the universes, who had come into the earth to be one of us, and show us what was possible.

When Mary heard this story, she looked deeply into my eyes and said, "You are blessed for what you have seen, Mary. Keep these stories close to your heart when the hard days come."

The Master's mother looked out the window when she said this—and at the time I did not understand the sadness in her eyes. She knew something I did not—even then—that the "hard days" would be harder than we ever could have imagined. I do not have the strength yet to write of those hard days, but I shall commit them to the written page before I am finished. For now, my friends, my foes, I wish to write of the wondrous happenings of our Lord and Master, Jesus, who became the Christ, and how those happenings changed my life and the lives of all those who knew him—and who *still* know him. As I have written aforetime, what God has ordained, not even death can be an obstacle. In the life of the Master, this too was true—it was a fact: Death did not stop his ministry, his legacy, and his promises that will live on forever. Though his mission was serious, and the Master was the first to per- fectly overcome all material trials and temptations and *become God while in the flesh*, he was still a man. He laughed, he drank wine, he loved children, he delighted in the beauties of nature. Even now I can see him in prayer in his secret place in the mountains—and I could *feel* that all creatures, all trees, all of life that lives in places seldom seen by human eyes in the forests, heard him—and the Creator I have no doubt was delighted to commune with the Master outside the confines of a build- ing that called itself a "church." For, as the Master often said, "God is

Spirit, and must be worshipped in Spirit. Wherever you find yourself drawn to commune with the Most High, go to that place, and within the stillness of your body and mind, your soul will be in communion with the Creator of All That Is. He took time to be all things to all people—be they of high estate or low, it did not matter to the Master. He saw all people as equal. And that gift he passed on to his Disciples and to all the people he met along the way, to all the people he healed. I cannot count the number of times I heard him whisper or say aloud to the masses, "Look for God in the eyes of every person you meet, regardless of their social position—for all are children of God. And as you seek to find God in all that you meet, it shall be so. The spiritual work, my brothers, my sisters, is trying to see the God–spirit in those who would revile you, or despise you, or hurt you. This is a work—but it is a noble one. It is the work of the Peaceful Warrior who chooses to move from the heart and forgive, rather than seek vengeance upon those who have wronged you. If you can forgive your executioner, you bear the mark of the highest calling. For those who would despise you are ignorant and know no better. Do not lower yourself to their standard, but work, my friends, work, to see the spark of the Divine even in them! This, this is the great secret that will set you free. Love the enemy. For it is the only weapon that will turn the tide of darkness into light. When you smile upon those who would despitefully use you, you then heap coals of fire upon their heads because they are expecting you to respond in kind!" After saying this, the Master laughed.

"Love your neighbor as yourself," he added, "for he *is* yourself. When you cross the bridge from this world into the next, you will see through the eyes and feel from the heart of all of the people you helped or hurt. This is no parable—this is a literal truth. So take time to be apart from the world and ask the Heavenly Father–Mother–God to give you strength to face your adversaries with love in your heart. Not for the outward appearance's sake, no, but for your soul's sake. For if you hate the neighbor who hates you, then you are wrapping yourselves in chains of darkness. Hatred breeds hatred. Love breeds love. Love overcomes hatred and is the only power that will bring Light out of the darkness."

Someone in the crowd asked the Master about his own enemies, and wanted to know what he was going to do about them.

He pondered upon this for a moment in silence and then a smile crept across his face. "I have my foes, yes. I have those who do not believe I am who I say I am. They are the ones who think they will silence my voice forevermore if they take my life—but they are mistaken. For he who gives up his life shall find it. For the words I speak unto you this day will be written upon the hearts of people everywhere. My enemies? They would have me put to death now if they could for they are afraid. I pity them, I do not feel hatred or anger toward them. I know they truly do not understand. Here is the essence of my message to you: People do hurtful things out of misunderstanding—they do not know that the evil they do will come back upon them tenfold. This is an immutable law. Likewise, the love you show forth to your fellow man will be multiplied an hundredfold and will live on in the souls of those not yet born. Even now my blood is upon the hands of my enemies, but they cannot touch my spirit—for my spirit is one with the Great Spirit. Remember this when the dark days come."

These are the words I recalled the Master speaking when I heard Mary speak of the "hard days" ahead. I had no idea, not an inkling of what would happen—and it may be too incredible for you to believe, but as I said in the beginning, I bear witness to all that I have seen, and it does not profit my soul one iota to fabricate these things.

At the time I heard the Master speaking about "death," I was certain that he was speaking in a parable, or a story. I had no idea he was speaking *literally*, that the dark forces would eventually take his life. I now know the Master was trying to prepare us for what was to come.

When the time came to enter into Jerusalem, many of the Disciples were overjoyed, for they thought, like many, that here Jesus would proclaim his kingdom. I did not share with Peter or James, or even John the feelings of foreboding I held in my heart. I kept this to myself. The night before we left, Martha held a banquet in her home and invited all the Disciples and friends of the Master.

I wanted in some way to show forth my love to the Master—for he had done so much for me. Before the banquet was served, I took special perfumed oil and I looked into the Master's eyes, not saying a word—only holding it out to him. The Master smiled and said, "As you wish,

Mary. As you would do a service unto me, you render a service unto God."

I knelt at the Master's feet and took his sandals off. I could sense the unease of some of the Disciples. Only Judas spoke aloud. He was always jealous of the closeness between the Master and myself. I paid him no heed, but poured the oil from an alabaster box, upon the Master's feet. I was overcome with emotion and my tears mingled with the oil.

"Mary," Judas said in a tone of reprimand, "why are you wasting that expensive oil? We could sell it for hundreds of pence, and give the money to the poor."

Judas had no sympathy for the poor—and the Master knew he was only finding fault with me because he could. The Master spoke to Judas.

"The poor you have with you always, Judas, and you can help them at anytime. You will not always have me with you. My time is short in this world, so leave Mary alone. She is anointing me for my burial." There was complete silence in the room. My tears multiplied when I heard his words—and they fell like rain upon the Master's feet. I had no cloth to dry them, so I wiped them away with my hair. I felt I had so little to offer this man who had given me so much. As he had done so often in the past, he read my thoughts, and I felt his hands upon each side of my face. He looked deep into eyes, my tear-stained face and the Master said, "Today, I say to all of you that wherever the Gospel of Love, Truth, and Light is preached of my passage through this world, this hour will be spoken of—and Mary shall be equally remembered and spoken of for the kindness she has given to me this day."

When I found the ability to speak again, I asked the Master a question.

"Master, do you speak in a parable when you say that I have anointed you for your burial?"

I cannot describe the expression on his beautiful face—sadness—the coming of an ancient promise to be fulfilled. Above all else, he looked upon me with a love so deep, so caring—it was a love I never wanted to be far from.

"Mary," the Master said, "have you not been with me so long that you do not know that death is an illusion? To become the butterfly, the caterpillar must first die. In its death, it becomes an illumined being—a beautiful winged creature. Though the time shall come when I shall lay down my life, I shall, by the grace of God, have my life be given back to me, in glorified form. Fear not, my dear one, fear not." I held his words close to my heart and my fears were gone—simply gone from me— about his trek to Jerusalem. For, as I looked into his eyes, it was as if I were looking into the eyes of God Himself. And this was true. He was the flesh incarnate of God. In that light, to what degree should I fear anything?

The next morning, as we were walking to Jerusalem—myself, the twelve Disciples, and many of the holy women who always prepared the way for his arrival into a new city—the Master told James and John to go into the city, to a small village called Bethphage and there they would find a donkey tied to a tree.

"If anyone questions you," the Master said, "tell them that I have need of her." They did what they were told and were awed once again by the Master's ability to foresee what his eyes could not see. They found the donkey exactly where the Master said it would be and the owner of her was standing by.

"The Master, Jesus, has need of her," John said.

The owner of the donkey said, "Yes, all is well. Take her with my blessing."

They brought her to the Master and he rode into Jerusalem on the back of a donkey, and the rest of us followed behind him. I could not believe the size of the throng that had gathered at the entrance of the city. There were multitudes of women and children welcoming the Master, and they laid palm leaves at his feet, along with flowers. They proclaimed the words that his Mother, Mary, had heard the night of his birth.

"Hosanna! Hosanna! Blessed is the king who comes in the name of the Lord! Peace on earth, good will to all men! Glory to God in the highest!" I saw a great light that descended from the heavens that shone upon the Master, and he smiled upon the masses and blessed them. There were also his enemies present, and they attempted to disperse the crowd who had come to welcome the Master, but to no avail. They tried to silence the crowd and Jesus said to them in a strong, powerful voice, "If those gathered here should hold their peace, the very stones would cry aloud in triumph for my coming!" This angered the Pharisees and high priests, and they stormed off. For the people who welcomed and blessed the Master far outnumbered those who were against him, and I heard one of the Pharisees say, with a great deal of bewilderment and anger, "The whole world is following him—who is he that would have such sway over the crowd?"

Jesus was at a great distance afar from the men who were saying such things—and when he reached them, he astonished them with his ability to know their thoughts, for he said to them, "Have you not heard that out of the mouths of babes comes perfect praise? They are praising the coming of Christ in their midst. *For I am He.*" The Pharisees stumbled away from the Master, astounded by the power in his voice and the illumination of his countenance as he entered the Holy City.

Again, my friends, I would remind you that those who did not understand the mission of Jesus believed that he had come to Jerusalem to cause dissension and set up his own kingdom. They understood not that his kingdom was one of Spirit, unseen by mortal eye.

As before, there were many of the crowd that had come to be healed—and he healed all that came to him—the halt, the blind, the lame were led to Jesus and he laid his hands upon them and they were healed. To some, the Master said, "Your sins are forgiven thee—go thy way, and be whole." Others he directed to show themselves to a priest and they would be healed.

In the midst of the air of celebration of the Master entering the city, I noticed that all were present except for Judas. I watched him conferring with some of the people who had rebuked the Master. I had always felt uneasy around Judas and I couldn't exactly say why. Looking back upon those days, there was a part of me that must have known that something dark was coming—but I had no idea that the majority of the darkness would be coming from Judas.

It was on the Passover eve that the Master, the Disciples, the mother of Jesus, and many others gathered for a banquet that had been arranged by an upright man named Nicodemus—he was of the orthodox faith but he had studied with the Master by night. Little did I know at the time that this would be the last time that I would be together with all of the Disciples and the Master. He did his best to prepare us for what was to take place, but we did not understand.

We were all seated at the table: the Disciples, the Master's Mother, several of the holy women and myself. There was placed before us boiled fish, rice with leeks, bread, and wine. The Master was dressed in the pearl-gray robe that had been made by Nicodemus' wife, and that was given to him by Nicodemus. It was gathered at the waist and it seemed to be perfectly formed—even as the Master himself. It is hard to describe the Master's countenance that night. I can still see his hair—a deep brown that was almost red, and tended to be curly—yet it flowed down to his shoulders and framed his beautiful face. He had long tapering fingers, with a longer fingernail on his left hand. His beard was closely cropped. Should I live to be a hundred years old, I'll never forget the steel-blue of his eyes. His stature was magnificent—powerful and strong. It was clear that he had spent years doing labor with his father, Joseph, as a carpenter.

I had the feeling that this was the last night we would all be together like this—and that thought filled me with sorrow. Yet, I remembered what the Master had taught me long ago, "Live for the moment—the here and now—and let tomorrow take care of itself." The Master was in good spirits, and he was laughing and telling stories. The story I remember that was the most humorous was when Peter and Andrew and the other Disciples were out on the sea, fishing.

"I could barely believe my eyes," John said. "Out of the early morning mist, there came the Master, walking upon the sea! Andrew asked, 'Is it a ghost? What is it?'" John looked upon the Master and smiled. "That's when the Master said, "Peace! Be not afraid! It is I!" Everyone was laughing at this point except for Peter, whose face had turned crimson.

"Will I never live this down?" Peter asked, looking skyward.

"No, Peter, you will not," said Jesus, laughing.

"Tell me what happened," I said. I knew the Master had performed amazing feats, but I had never heard a tale of him *walking upon water!*

John continued. "When Peter saw it was the Master, walking upon the sea as if he were walking on dry land, he said, 'Master! If it is you, may I come out and join you?' And the Master said, 'If that is your wish, join me.' And Peter tentatively stepped onto the water from the side of the boat and was astonished to find himself upon it! He went running over to the Master, and not a drop of water soaked his sandals!"

"I could never swim a stroke," Peter said. "You've no idea the courage it took me to follow you out there, Master." At this point, Peter himself was laughing.

"I think it was at that point," the Master said, "that Peter allowed his smaller mind to take over. As soon as he thought, 'This is impossible,' he immediately plunged into the icy waters!"

"I can still see that in my memory as if it happened yesterday," Andrew said. "All at once Peter began shouting and splashing about, yelling, 'Save me! Save me! I'm drowning!'" Laughter filled the room.

I looked over at Jesus who was also laughing, shaking his head at the memory.

"What did you do?" I asked Jesus.

"First of all, I laughingly said, 'Oh Peter! Oh what a small amount of faith you have!' I told him to let go of his preconceived ideas and beliefs and believe that he was standing right next to me. In the next instant, he rose out of the water and held onto me as if I were his lifeline!"

"You were," Peter said. "Indeed you were!"

"As we walked back to the boat," the Master said, "Peter kept trying to hold onto the idea that all things are possible with God, and then he would think, 'This is impossible!' Just as soon as the thought crossed his mind, *splash!*"

The room roared with laughter. "How many times did he descend into the seas and rise again to the surface before he reached the boat?" Andrew asked.

"Oh, seven or eight times, I would wager," the Master said.

"Only three times!" Peter protested, laughing. "Only three times did I allow my mind to get in the way! Then I was safely on board the boat."

When the laughter died down, the Master looked about the room.

"I have some things to share with you, my friends," the Master said, his tone turning serious. "The mind is as vast as the sea. There are depths and heights beneath the surface, unseen by mortal man. There are life forms that cannot be fathomed—that are created by the mind. We call them thoughts—but they are living things—and thoughts must find manifestation in the material world at some point in time. Know this: Each soul is as a thought in the mind of God—hence they are eternal, imbued with all the creative powers of the Father–Mother–God.

"For this reason did I come into the earth—to show man what was possible when the mind of man is melded, at-one, with the mind of the Creator. As the Divine mind is limitless, so is the mind of the human creature. But through the passage of eons of time, the souls of men and women forgot their limitlessness. What you have seen me do, and the things you will see me do in the days to come, may appear miraculous or impossible. But they are neither magical or tricks of illusion.

"The things I do, you one day will also do. Believe—believe my brothers and my sisters—that you are not tied to the earth, blown hither and thither by the winds of chance, without purpose or direction—but are guided and directed—always—by the Divine Creator. Even when things seem at their lowest point, or you feel you are without hope, call upon me and I will come to you quickly. In a little while you shall see me seldom for the remainder of your lives. But know that my Spirit, which is at-one with the Spirit of God, will always be with you.

"Remember that the Divine Mind of God is limitless, and you are a child of God, hence you too have limitless powers. Pray, and enter the sanctuary of your own deeper Self, the tabernacle of the Most High within, and there ask what you will. And believing, it shall be done unto you.

"When the hard days come, know that there is no wrong road or turn upon the path of the spiritual life. It is true that the path to the Heavenly world of God is narrow and straight, but all roads lead to this path—and I will guide you the whole way. When hardships befall you—know that these come not as punishments—for God in His infinite mercy and grace knows only love for His creations, His children—you. But in order for a tree to bear more fruit, it must be pruned. So it is with all of us who inhabit the earth. The trials, the struggles, the turmoil—these are but purgings of the soul that it may bring forth more fruitful deeds. So banish from your thoughts the idea that 'this or that has come upon me because God is seeking retribution for my misdeeds.' God seeks nothing of the kind. There is a law—and it is a beneficent law—the law of balance. That which is hurled forth into the ethers in the form of wishes, desires, whether they be for upliftment or destruction, these must return to the sender in the form of fulfillments—be it in the present life or in the next.

"Hence, show compassion, kindness, patience, love, forgiveness, to your fellow man—for that which ye sow, is what you will reap—in this world, or in the next. So be patient even with your enemies—for they know not what they do—and as you forgive others, you too will be forgiven by God. If you refuse to forgive and hold grudges, then you do so to your own undoing."

There was silence around the table as the group took in and pondered the Master's words. Then he broke bread into pieces and handed a piece to every one seated at the table. Then he poured wine in a beautiful chalice.

"These are emblems that I give to all of you, that you will remember me. The bread represents my body—the glorified body. The wine represents my blood—the lifeblood of the living God. Take and eat of this bread, drink of this wine, and as you do, know that you are part of the blessed Covenant—the Covenant that the Father–Mother–God dwells within you—and will never leave you."

At this point a strange thing happened. He looked over at Judas and said, "What you must do, Judas, do it quickly." Without pause, Judas lowered his head, stood, and left the room.

The Master then passed the chalice around the table and each of us drank from it. "My friends, do this in remembrance of me, and all that we shared together. It is a sacred bond that shall never be broken."

The Master then asked the Disciples to be seated in a row back from the table where he could walk in front of them. He went into another room and came out with a basin and a pitcher and a cloth. He asked all the Disciples to remove their sandals. As he knelt by Peter with the basin of water and the pitcher, Peter said, "No, Master, I cannot allow you to wash my feet."

"Peter, he who is the greatest among you," Jesus said, "shall be the servant of all. These are words given to me from the all-knowing Creator. Would you have me deny His purposes for me?"

"You may wash my legs, too," Peter said. At that everyone laughed.

The Master washed all the Disciples feet and said prayers for each of them as he came to them. I was again moved to tears by this mighty, gentle soul, this living Messiah, who would humble himself before us in such a beautiful manner.

When Judas departed, I knew that the end was near—but in my heart I knew it was not the end, but it was a beginning. No one knows the role they must play in the universal scheme of things, and though there would be dark days ahead, I kept telling myself that it is the darkest before the dawn.

The Master walked over to his Mother and kissed her cheek. Then he came to me and kissed my forehead, and my left and right cheeks. "God will always be with you, Lady Magdalene," he said.

"And also with you, my Beloved, always," I said, and stood to embrace him. He held me like a small child is embraced by its parent—and again I felt like I'd come home.

Jesus then went to sit by a harp that was in the corner of the room. We all gathered around him.

"Let us sing a psalm, my friends, then let us depart from here—for time is short.

Our voices filled the night as he beautifully played the harp—and I sensed angels and Divine spirits roundabout us as we sang the ancient words of David:

"He that dwelleth in the secret place of the most High shall abide under the shadow of the Almighty. I will say of the Lord, He is my refuge and my fortress: my God, in him will I trust.

"Surely he shall deliver thee from the snare of the fowler, and from the noisome pestilence.

"He shall cover thee with his feathers, and under his wings shalt thou trust: His truth shall be thy shield and buckler . . .

"There shall no evil befall thee, neither shall any plague come nigh thy dwelling.

"For he shall give his angels charge over thee, to keep you in all thy ways.

"They shall bear thee up in their hands, lest thou dash thy foot against a stone.

"Thou shalt tread upon the lion and adder: the young lion and the dragon shalt thou trample under feet.

"Because he hath set his love upon me, therefore will I deliver him: I will set him on high, because he hath known my name.

"He shall call upon me, and I will answer him: I will be with him in trouble, I will deliver him, and honor him.

"With long life will I satisfy him, and show him my salvation."

The Master finished playing the harp and I swore I could hear angels singing from above the place where we dwelt. I looked into the eyes of the Master and there was joy and sadness. He stood, beckoned his mother to walk at his right side, and me at his left. He put his arms around us and we all descended the stair to the night air.

"Come," Jesus said, "It is finished."

We walked to the Garden of Gethsemane.

8

The Arrest and Crucifixion of Jesus

Now the time has come for me to tell the hardest part of the journey of my Beloved—the Master—and his journey through the darkest night of his soul. He tried to tell us, to warn us, of what was to come, but we could not comprehend. The Master led us all to the Mount of Olives after the supper. As I had always dreamed, I walked by him side-by-side, and he took my hand in his, and he kissed it, leading me a short distance away from the friends and Disciples.

"Be strong, Mary," the Master said. "The hard days are coming—but they will pass swiftly. I have much to tell you, but the time is not yet. Just be strong for my sake." I felt a cold feeling within me, and some unnameable fear. I suddenly embraced him, never wanting to let him go.

"Master," I whispered, "there is much I do not understand. Please give me the strength I need, and the understanding."

Tears flowed down my face and upon his shoulder. He held me tightly. I've never felt so loved, so complete . . . I knew I was being held by the Living God made flesh. I released him and looked into the eternity of his eyes. My own eyes were blurry with tears. I could see the Disciples milling about a short distance away, stealing glances our way, and whispering amongst themselves.

"Not long from now, Mary, you will understand all things," the Master said, smiling. "One cannot rush the blooming of a rose. All things will become clear in due season."

Those words quelled the fear in me. And we walked to a clearing in Olivet. The Master bid the Disciples—all except Judas, who had gone from us—to come close and listen to him.

"Lo," the Master said, "the days will come when you shall be hauled into the courts—you will be stoned, you will be beaten in the synagogues—you will stand condemned before the rulers of this world, and governors and kings will sentence you to death. But you will falter not, and you will testify for truth and righteousness—and I shall be there with you, my friends. You shall not bear these things alone."

I looked about the gathering of the Disciples, the friends, and his Blessed Mother, who sat by his side. All were silent. I watched as Mary wiped away a tear, and I wondered in my heart, what he was trying to say. What meaning was there to this parable? I hoped against hope that it was a parable—but in my heart I knew it was not. The Master was giving us a prophecy, a foretelling of what was to come. I wanted to run away, cover my ears, and hear no more. But as I gazed into the Master's steel-blue eyes, I saw serenity, and a peace that cannot be described filled me. I know the Master knew my thoughts, just as he knew all the thoughts of all the people surrounding him. I did not know what was coming, but I knew it was going to be as a raging storm.

"In those hours of trial, my beloved ones," the Master said, "be not anxious for what you will say. You will not need to think of what to say—for lo, the Holy Breath of God will overshadow you and give you the words to say. My spirit shall be with you, always, the whole way, and you will not be afraid. For I shall travel this hard road before you—and where I must go, you too must follow—if you would truly be a follower of mine."

"Master, pray, tell us, when will these days come upon us, and what is this hard road you must travel?" Peter asked. "Do you speak to us in a parable? How can we understand—"

The Master lifted his hand and silenced Peter, a smile playing across his lips. "Peter, I know you have so many questions in your heart. I ask you only to listen and the answers will come—in due time. The hour will come when you yourself will deny that you ever knew me." There was shocked silence, and Peter gasped.

"Master," Peter said, when he could find his voice again, "such a day will never come. Never. I would never deny you." Tears rolled down his burly cheeks.

"This is not meant as something to cause you pain, Peter," the Master said. "All is well. It is destined and so it shall be—before the cock crows three times tomorrow morning—you will deny me."

"Never," Peter said, shaking his head violently. "I have seen—"

"Silence," the Master said, not unkindly, looking upon Peter with great compassion and . . . yes—with sadness—even though the Master's smile never wavered.

As I have said, I did not understand so many things at the time that I now understand. The rest of the Disciples looked upon Peter as if he had a plague—and there was disgust painted upon their faces.

"My friends," the Master said, "do not look upon Peter in such a manner. For all of you will be scattered like sheep without a shepherd before this night is through, *and all of you will deny me in your own way*. Know this is already destined, so be not anxious, nor worried. I tell you these things before they come to pass so that you will know of them, when the dark hours come. Be of good cheer—for I, the first of many, have overcome the world. Though the earth be broken up, though nation shall rise against nation, though Jerusalem shall be turned to rubble, though the very earth shall go through many trials and tribulations— the words which I speak, are from the Father–Mother–God. And they shall not pass away."

"Master," John said, deeply grief-stricken, "you speak as if you were leaving us—and this I cannot bear. I will follow you to the ends of the earth."

"John," the Master said, "where I go, you cannot follow—not yet. I go to the Father, from whence I came. I go to prepare a place for you that where I am there you will be also. Let not your heart be troubled, John, neither let it be sad or afraid. You believe in God, believe also in me."

"We do not know where you intend to go," Thomas said. "How can we know the way?

"Thomas," the Master said, "I *am* the way, the truth, and the life. I manifest the Christ of God—which is the love of God made manifest to you—right now, right here."

At that point, it was like a stream of great light came from the heavens and illumined the Master—we all saw it—and marveled. "Behold, the Father sends a sign to each of you, that you might know the truth. Abide in me, and do the works that God, through me, has taught you how to do, and you will bear much fruit, and God will honor you as he has honored me. For it is not me who has wrought the miraculous wonders you have seen—but it is the Father–Mother–God that dwells within me. All these things that you have seen me do have been given to me—*through me*, greater things than these shall you do, for I am the first of the many. The things that you have seen me do, you have been witness to the glory of God, working through man. Of myself, I can do nothing, but it is God who works through me that brings forth the miraculous things you have been witness to."

Many of the people, including myself had so many questions, but the Master stood and looked down with compassion and complete love and said, "There is much more that I have yet to tell you, but not now. For my time here is short. The time has come for me to tell you that the hour has come when you will be scattered like sheep, and every one of you will be afraid. But again, I say, be not afraid. The time is shortly coming when I shall be left alone, but I shall not be alone, for the Father–Mother–God will be with me the whole way.

"Those who do not comprehend the light which I have sought to manifest are coming—and these wicked ones will take me to the judgment seat of their courts, and in the presence of the multitudes I will give up my life—a pattern for you, and the generations to come, to follow. But I will rise again and come to you. I speak of these things so that when the Son of Man is betrayed, you will know and be not afraid, nor bewildered. I will return to you—remember that—no matter what happens or what you see—*I will return to you.* Be of good cheer, I have overcome the world."

With that, the Master turned and walked to a clearing in the Mount of Olives and He bid farewell to his mother, with a kiss, and I could hear a pleading in her voice. My heart went out to her because she did not want to let go of her beloved son. But I know that he quenched the fear in her heart, just as one would douse a fire with cool water—and her fear was replaced with serenity. How many times I had seen him do this for so many people! For when she walked away with her friend Sophie, her daughter Ruth, and the other women who had prepared the feast, she walked with her head held high. The mother of the greatest spiritual warrior the world has ever known went her way.

"Watch with me, my friends, while I pray," the Master said, as he knelt upon the ground.

The Disciples looked at one another and sat down in the grove, leaning against the trees and rocks. The Master wanted to be alone to pray. Even so, I was drawn near to him, just as the waves are drawn to the shore. I kept my distance, but I could hear the Master's words—and my heart was rent within me, for this was the *man* Jesus—who was about to face the greatest challenge of his life. It took all of my strength not to run to him.

"My Father-God, the hour has come. The son of man must now be lifted from the earth, and may he falter not, that the world may know the power of sacrifice. I came to do thy will, O God, and in thy sacred name, the Christ is glorified, that men may see the Christ as life, as light, as love, as truth. And through the Christ become themselves the life, the light, the love, the truth. I praise thy name because of these whom thou hast given me, for they have honored thee and they will honor thee. None of them are lost, and none are gone away, except the blinded son of carnal life, who hath gone forth to sell his Lord, and be the one that will enable all things to come to pass, even as it was prophesied."

At this point, there was a breaking in the Master's voice, and his hands were tightly clenched against his forehead, and sweat began to pour down his face and soak his tunic. In horror, I watched the sweat turn to blood—I choked back a sob by biting my knuckle. I prayed for him, the Master, even as he prayed for us. Oh, how I loved him! And wanted so much to comfort him and could not. My tears fell like rain, my heart was breaking. I longed to comfort him, but could not—it was like there was an invisible barrier that kept me from going to him. So I stayed in my place, wept silently, and heard the Master's voice cry out.

"Father! Now, I come to thee, and am no more in this mortal life. Keep thou these men and women to whom I have made known thy wisdom, thy love, thy truth. Glorify thy son, O God, with the love I had with thee before the worlds were. And if it be thy will . . . let . . . this . . . cup . . . pass . . . from . . . me." I heard a sob, a sigh, and with a deep breath, in a loud voice the Master cried out, "Nevertheless, not my will, O God, but thine be done—in me and through me. I am thine. Give thou me the strength to endure the hours until I see thee face to face."

In agony he prayed. The strain upon his human form was great. His veins were burst asunder and his brow was bathed in sweat and blood. He turned to his Disciples who were sleeping. I could see how this wounded his soul, his spirit.

"Couldn't you watch with me for one hour?" the Master said, in a loud voice, rousing the Disciples. "I am wrestling with a powerful foe—fear—and yet you sleep?" He shook his head and went back to his place of prayer, where he fell upon the ground

"I know the spirit is alert and willing, but the flesh is weak, O God," the Master said. "If I must drink of this bitter cup, give me the strength of body, as I have the strength of soul—you, O Father, have given this to me. My human self is afraid. Take this from me—and let me lay down my life so that I may take it up again to show what mankind may do. This is my prayer. Hear me, O God, in my hour of need, and be thou near unto me, that I may glorify thy Spirit in the earth—and show mortal man what is possible."

Again, he walked back and the Disciples were sleeping. The sadness shown in his face and I saw, for the first time, disappointment in his face—no anger—no rage, only sadness and disappointment. He woke John, his most beloved Disciple and said, "With all the love you have for me, could you not watch with me for a single hour?" John began to sob. I thought the Master sought to head to the clearing where he prayed but he walked to where I was standing. I felt ashamed at first, but the look in his eyes shone otherwise. He took me gently by the hand and led me to the Disciples and said:

"She has stood watch for me. As I have said, wherever the Gospel of the Living God in man is preached in the generations to come, Mary Magdalene's name will be remembered and honored."

I write this here not for my own glory, but because in that moment, I could feel that the old self, the old Mary Magdalene, was finally dead and gone—I was—in that moment—fully changed to the woman who writes these words.

The Master turned his face to me and said, "Mary of Magdalene, you are, and ever shall be from this day forward, the thirteenth Disciple."

He kissed me upon the forehead and went back to pray. "Watch for me, for just a short time longer," the Master said. The Disciples looked bewildered, as if they had partaken of strange wine. It was as if they could not stay awake. And as soon as the Master went back to pray, they fell into their stupor, their sleep.

He walked away and again, fell upon his knees and prayed with all his might—the flesh battling the Spirit. I could only imagine the pain the Master was feeling—but suddenly there was a ceasing of turmoil in his soul. It came after the Master again said, "Not my will, but thine be done." The heavenly light we had seen earlier was now beaming down upon the Master—and there were legions of angels that came round about him. I saw the astonishment upon his beautiful face—and the angels lifted him to a standing position and they wiped away the blood and the sweat. This I saw with my own eyes—it does not matter if those who read these words do not believe—but I know in my heart it happened and in that moment I knew beyond any doubt that this was the Son of God. I watched him spread his arms wide, his head thrown back, a look of ecstasy upon the Master's face. The glowing angels of the Holy Light bowed down to him and I could see them removing the fear, the anxiety—all that had been humanly afraid in him.

"Thank you, Father," the Master said, "Keep these blessed ones thou hast committed unto me—and protect them that they may bear witness to the wonders Thou hast performed. As I am one with thee, and thou art one with me, may they—all those who believe—be one with us, that all of the world may know that thou has sent me forth to do thy will. Love them as thou hast loved me."

The Master arose and went to where the Disciples lay. His mood had changed like a summer storm to a spring breeze. He took a deep breath.

"Arise my friends," the Master said in a loud voice, "For the time has come where the Son of Man is to be delivered to the enemies of the Light. Remember all that I told you."

Moments later there was a rustling through the trees and I saw torches and men carrying swords and weapons of all sorts. I was not shocked to see the horde was being led by Judas Iscariot.

"Behold," the Master said, "the betrayer of the Son of Man leads the way." The Master walked to meet them. "Whom do you seek?" the Master asked the well-dressed man of the Sanhedrin who was behind Judas.

"We seek the man of Galilee," the high priest, Caphias, said. "The man called Jesus, who calls himself the Son of God."

The Master answered, "*I am he*," and then raised his hands into the air and the entire olive grove was filled with ethereal light. Most of Caphias' horde screamed and backed away from the Master, quickly running back the way they had come. I could hardly suppress a smile. Even Judas fell back a few steps. Only the bravest of soldiers stayed with Caphais. When he spoke again, the priest's voice was quivering.

"We seek the man called Jesus," the priest said.

"I told you before, I am *He*." This time, the entire ground seemed to quake beneath their feet. The priest fell down and, it was no surprise to see Judas helping him up. Judas walked forward, and, as a sign to the priest, he kissed the Master, gently holding his face in his hands. "This is the man," Judas said.

"You would betray your master with a kiss, Judas?" the Master said, a smile playing across his lips. "This thing must need be done, but woe to him who does betray his Lord. Your carnal self has overshadowed your spiritual self and you know little of what you have done. But in a little time your conscience will assert itself, and in remorse, lo, you will take your own life."

Whispering, Judas said to the Master, "No, Master, no! That's not what I meant. I've done this so you can show them who you truly are!"

"Oh, Judas," the Master said, shaking his head. "The Kingdom is not one that was to be established on earth, as a government, or rulership, it is *within*. Change that which is within, and the outer will follow." The Master laid his hand on Judas' cheek. "Poor Judas."

To Judas' astonishment, Jesus walked forward to the priests, where they quickly snared him and bound his arms and hands in ropes and chains behind his back.

"Why do you behave in such a manner?" the Master asked. Coming here in the middle of the night with swords and clubs and chains, as if I were a robber! I sat daily in the Temple teaching, but you did not take me. But this is your hour and the power of darkness, that the Scriptures of the prophets may be fulfilled.

"Have I not healed your sick? Those that were once blind have received their sight and those who were deaf can now hear, can they not? You could have come for me on any day, in any public place. I will go with you, but this—these chains—are unnecessary."

The Master looked heavenward, uttered a prayer and the chains and ropes fell from his arms, landing upon the ground in a heap. The guards were astonished. Again, I couldn't help but stifle a smile. Even in the worst of situations, the Master had the ability to be humorous.

"There," the Master said, "that's better." The guards were searching the grounds for the Disciples—and the Master said, "You have no business with anyone but me. Leave them alone."

That was not difficult because there wasn't a friend or ally in sight. The Disciples had, as the Master prophesied, been scattered abroad.

"Mary," the Master said. "Go to my mother's house. Do not be afraid—all will be well." One of the guards leaped forward and slapped the Master's face.

"Do not speak unless we direct you to," the guard said. Caphias looked satisfied. "Take him to Pilate's Court."

I took my chances and moved forward quickly and kissed the Master on the cheek. "I love you, Master."

"Be not afraid, Mary," the Master said, as they led him away. "You'll understand everything in due time."

The guard that slapped him stepped forward to hit him again. Caphias stopped him. "Enough," Caphias said. "Be gone from here, harlot," Caphias said to me. I knew then that I had fully changed—for his insult did not affect me at all. The Master gave me the gift of serenity and peace. How often I used to jump and attack people verbally at the least provocation! Truly, the demons that had once inhabited me were gone. Yes, the Mary of Magdalene who once dined with Roman royalty, who had beautiful lovers, who wore the finest clothing from Persia, who harbored so much darkness within—she was gone. Even when I looked at Judas, I felt no hatred, only pity. He did not understand. I have no doubt that he expected the Master to disappear from his enemies in the grove. The Master had done it so many times before. But this time . . . well . . . the Master was taken into custody. As I said before, I did not understand. And so, I fled to Mother Mary's home. It took me some time to get there, but as I did, I found John, Peter, Andrew—all of the Disciples were gathered in Mary's home. John was in tears, and Mary had her arms around his shoulders. He was describing what happened—and there was not a dry eye in the house.

"I suspect the Dark Forces, which despised the Master, swirled its paralyzing forces around us, clouded our minds and *put us to sleep*. For I found myself falling asleep even after I heard him utter the words for us to stay on guard and on watch! Oh, Mary, I fell asleep—may God forgive me. And what is worse, I ran away! We left the Master when he was most alone—the only hour he asked anything of us. 'Watch with me for an hour,' he said. Those words will forever haunt me. We—I—slept while he, our beloved, lay bleeding, pleading, praying—his human self struggling with his spirit self to the very end. May God forgive me. Now I know how badly he agonized in that Garden of Gethsemane. Alone, he prayed—alone he was afraid and was without ally, in the darkest night of the soul. And we slept in the very darkness the Master wrestled to overcome."

"He was not alone, John," Mary said. "He was with God—and it was, in many ways, the ultimate test of his Messiahship. He had no allies, no friends, no one—it was between my son and the unseen God."

Mary took a deep shuddering breath. I could see the tears in her eyes. And there was also a look about her as if . . . it's difficult to explain . . . as if she knew this day would come.

"My son was completely human and yet completely at one with God," Mary said. "But he was not beyond being human. That is the great paradox."

"But Mary," Andrew said, "This was the man, who had wept with Martha and Mary over Lazarus. Bleeding in the Garden was the man who had compassion and wept and returned Lazarus from the dead. The Master had done this so that the world would know that God speaks and works wonders through humankind. But more than that, he called upon the Forces out of compassion so that the family would not be bereaved—out of compassion he called Lazarus from death."

The tears were also flowing from Andrew, "This is the man I abandoned. This was the same man who saved us from certain death during a violent storm at sea. He spoke to the storm with the power and voice once given only to the mighty Archangel Michael, the holy warrior of God. Your son was the first of the mortals who commanded the elements to be still. In a moment, that storm recognized its Maker, and instantly the destructive winds became a calm summer wind! Even Michael bowed and obeyed the Master's voice."

"All the more reason that we needn't fear, Andrew," Mary said. "You must realize, that what is happening is the will of God. Else my son would have disappeared. I cannot say I understand fully—but I know that his entire life was a Divine Gift—to me—and to the countless others he helped, healed, and to whom he ministered. So now, I must not doubt. I must banish fear—and I know that whatever my son is going through, he is going through with the full awareness of God."

Mary took John's face in her hands. "I want you to renounce this guilt. And let your mind remember him at the happiest times. This man, who is my son, loved to dance and he sang and loved children. Remember him turning the water into wine? Oh, what a fine celebration! He danced with the bride, and we danced with hilarity and joy and passed the night and into the dawn. Peculiar, but his wine was the only spirits I have ever partaken of that did not leave me feeling lethargic in the morning light. I believe now that wine was the grapes of his Spirit." She echoed my own words, written about the wedding feast.

I smiled at the memory. Here we were, and the Mother of the Master was lending *us* comfort!

Everyone was wondering why Judas did what he did—in betraying the Master. I shared with them my own view that poor, ignorant Judas, thought that the kingdom of which the Master spoke was a political position that would overthrow Rome!

"He didn't understand," I said. "Judas had seen the Master disappear when the crowds set to lay hands upon him, or to hurt him, and I know that when he kissed the Master, he expected the Master would vanish like a phantom. I hoped in my heart that the Master would! If he had, then Caphias and the high priests would have to believe that the Master *was* the Messiah."

Everyone gathered knew of the Master's arrest, yet none believed for a moment the high priests could hold him for long. As I said, the Master had the power from On High. We hoped beyond hope that the Master would return soon. Only Mary, the Blessed Mother, was as still as a deer who freezes the moment she sees the hunter fire his deadly arrow and remains unmoved. She stood at the doorway, looking out toward Jerusalem. She stood alone, the familiar blue veil covering her head—she was like a statue among us—standing at the doorway—a mother longing for her son.

John told the Master's mother that he would go with a messenger to obtain any information. I sat with the Master's brothers and sister, James, Jude, and Ruth, and the Disciples. While John and the messenger went to Jerusalem, Mary quietly sat in prayer and deep meditation. I knew that she possessed many of the gifts of the spirit her son possessed. The hours passed slowly. Moments before Mary came back to waking consciousness, John and the messenger returned.

Mary did not hurry to the door as the rest of us did—she stayed in her chair, head bowed. After I heard the terrible news, I realized that Mary must have followed John in spirit. John walked into her room and knelt at her feet and took her hand in his.

"Mary . . . I . . . I don't know how to say this . . . "

"You do not have to, my son," Mary said to John. "I know that my son is going forth to Golgotha. I must follow him." Mary looked at the floor and he put his arm around her. "Please tell the others what is happening," Mary said.

John explained to all of us that Jesus had been found guilty of trumped up charges, and he was condemned to die, execution by crucifixion. Ruth, James, and Jude went to the Master's mother, and they all held each other and wept. I couldn't believe it. I simply couldn't believe this was happening. I felt like I was in a nightmare, a terrible dream from which I wished I could awaken.

Mary stood and walked into the sitting room where all were gathered. Some of the Disciples said they would defend him, fight for him, die for him if necessary.

"We will not allow this to happen without a fight," Peter said.

"Peter," Mary said, "sit down." Peter immediately found a place to sit. All eyes were upon dear sweet Mary. Ever since the Master chose the Disciples, Mary was always the Mother to these wayward, but good-hearted fisherman. Mary commanded all of the Disciples to listen to her closely.

"The dark ones know my son has left his teachings with you," Mary said. "They will kill you if you are seen with me. Walk far behind me. Should you be questioned—if you love me and my son—then you will obey and deny you know or *ever knew me or my beloved son*. You are his life now—and you will be his messengers after this awful night. The legacy must be passed from you to the next generations and for the coming New Race. There was a reason you left my son in the Garden. Had you not, you would have been arrested with him. My sons, my daughters, listen to me carefully:

"If you seek to comfort me on the road to Golgotha, in this dark travail, you will betray my son, his love, and the legacy of the Most High. Only John is to walk with me—and Mary Magdalene, and the companion women who have been with me since the beginning. To John, my son must give further teachings. Yes, even *more* must he give to his beloved Disciple this night—even in the last hours of his physical life. Wait until we have passed over the hills, my sons, before you step foot from this door. And do not interfere nor intervene—for his sake, and for my love."

We wept, and she held us. They all promised her they would walk apart even while their hearts were breaking. How could this woman even think beyond the horror that was upon her? How could a mother think of their safety while her son was being beaten and whipped even as he bore the weight of the cross he would be nailed upon? How? Because she was—and ever shall be—the mother of all the earth's children. She had strength unseen—and her strength was given to endure this—the depths of agony—by the blessed strength of Archangel Michael, I have no doubt. I can only imagine how the Disciples felt—having to walk apart from her in the darkest hour.

"Promise me," Mary said. "Promise me you will walk apart from me and not interfere." Each of the Disciples promised. And so, I took Mary's arm, John walked on the other side, and we made our way to the streets of Jerusalem. She walked not as a martyr, but as a woman—the Holy Mother of earth itself—who was forever giving birth, forever burying her children.

I tried to imagine what the Disciples were going through. At least I was there to lend some comfort to Mary. But the others—how difficult it must have been to walk apart and hide their faces from her! That, my friends, must have been the most agonizing of all. How can a child watch the suffering of its mother and not run to her? Peter later told me that he was able to walk apart from the blessed Mother only by repeating the words she said, " . . . you must remain . . . to write my son's legacy . . . you will betray me if you even acknowledge you know me." Oh, that terrible night! We watched the terrible drama of the Master walking to his death up the hill of Golgotha, all the while being beaten and hurt and ridiculed by the soldiery.

The crowds were crammed in the narrow streets of Jerusalem, and we pushed our way through until we saw . . . him—the Master. I cannot adequately describe the scene. There were those who were weeping, some people were ridiculing him, the soldiers were flaying him with barbed whips. He was carrying the cross-beam of the cross on his shoulders.

The Master's own Mother could not comfort her son, any more than we could comfort her. I do not know how, but I drew moments of strength from some unseen Force while the Master's blood was trampled in footprints behind him. I saw . . . I witnessed . . . and my only comfort was holding onto the Blessed Mother. God forgive me, I prayed, that the end of the world was near. Mary rested her head on John's shoulder as we walked, and I had my arm around her waist. John and I looked at one another at one point and it all seemed so unreal. One day, we were celebrating at Cana, watching the sick being healed by the Master, and now . . . he was going to this cruel death. It was beyond comprehension.

It felt like the end of the world.

Indeed the world and perhaps worlds would have ended . . . had the Master not defied the dark ones and conquered death. If the Master himself had not embraced me with his powerful arms, and blessed me, I could not, would not, live to face another dawn. But yes, he came back to us, and I understood fully only then, when he showed himself to all of us after the third day, when we laid him in the tomb. I will write more of that soon. For now, I must get through reliving this terrible night, for my strength is waning.

In the dark night of every soul—the lonely Garden of Gethsemane—it is forbidden to know the Holy Secret: A Disciple must be fully human and know the depths in order to know the heights—and become a fully awakened spiritual master, just like the Master. How can one ever recognize the light if there is no dark night before it? The dark night of the soul leads the soul to seek for the Eternal Light. A mystery few can grasp or accept—but it is true—it is the Master's legacy.

I kept my eyes upon Mary when the pain was too great for me to watch them beat the Master while he carried his cross. Her countenance was the purity and innocence of a lily on that road to Golgotha. Her beauty was so out of place in that damnable place—like a sacred flower in a lovely vase—fragile and vulnerable—and that beauty and grace and innocence was the light in the darkest place of the world on that day.

Later, after the Resurrection, Mary shared with me a sacred vision she had on that awful road to Golgotha. She said she could feel the powerful presence of Archangel Michael's surrounding her—giving her strength to endure and go on.

"Such knowledge might seem to hold no comfort in such a dark hour," Mary said. "But knowing that God had sent one of His most powerful emissaries to me—Michael the great Archangel—who sustained my heart from ceasing to beat. I felt as if I walked with legions of angels behind me. You and John were the angels beside me." She smiled at me—the most beautiful smile—I knew she never lost her faith—even as her son went to his death—somehow she knew that he was the One, the first One, to conquer death.

Mary appeared fragile and delicate—but she had a heart of gold, the strength of a thousand warriors. Who else could witness what she saw and not fall apart. She did not. There were tears, but she remained. Such strength and courage . . . I cannot imagine. How does a parent watch the brutal death of her son? As I said, Mary, the mother of the Master was, and always will be, the mother of the mightiest warrior the world has ever known. Jesus was—and is—a revolutionary—a warrior of the heart.

I watched as soldiers removed the beam and placed it on the vertical wooden piece that would make the cross. I watched as they laid him upon it and pounded the nails into his hands and feet. He made no sound, but only arched his back upon that terrible tree. I saw his lips murmuring in prayer and he seemed to be far away from the horror that was happening. I wept, but Mary did not. She only held my hand tighter as they upended the cross, and put it in a hole that was dug to hold it upright. We were standing within a few feet of the Master. John dropped to his knees and wept. I was astonished for he spoke to his mother as if the pain was bearable. In my mind, I couldn't fathom such a thing:

"Mother, Mary, I must die in order to live," the Master said. "You must endure to be the eternal Mother of generations not yet born. You must persevere to be the mother of a race of benevolent warriors. It is ordained, my Mother . . . this is but the passing of shadows, and will be mercifully swift. Keep the faith. I love you . . . and will be with you . . . always."

When he started to speak, John rose to his feet and he smiled at him.

"John," the Master said. "Be a son to my mother in my stead. Mother, Mary, be a mother to him in my place. And remember, where two or more of you gather, there am I in the midst of you."

I wondered if my eyes were playing tricks upon me. Could it be that he was smiling? No . . . he truly was. I saw the Master's face looking upon all those who gathered at the cross and he was smiling. Smiling! In that smile, my friends, his beauty could be seen like a beacon, shining through the dust and blood and that terrible crown of thorns they cruelly placed upon his head. His light and beauty shown through the blood and hurt and sweat upon his face.

He smiled with joy just as he did when he played with little children. I thought my eyes betrayed me. I moved cautiously forward and thought I'd seen an illusion. But it was true. My God, my Master, was beaming like a thousand candles in the darkest night. Dear merciful God, he was not only smiling—but . . . grinning. I understood then why the soldiers had so savagely beaten him with the barbed leather straps, mercilessly tearing chunks of flesh from his body. The innocence and beauty of his smile to his mother, to me, to John, to Sophie, and the friends who had gathered at the crucifixion never wavered! He turned his face to the left, to the right, and his eyes were alight with mirth, merriment—and . . . yes . . . with good humor. And he looked at all who walked apart from Mary—the Disciples. And as I turned, I could feel that the Disciples no longer felt the guilt and remorse for running away. He forgave them and loved them. It was a palpable feeling—love. There were two others who had been crucified, that were on either side of the Master.

The man on his left said, "If you are who they say you are, the Messiah, why don't you come down from the cross?"

Jesus smiled at him and said, "That would ruin the finale."

"And what exactly is that going to be?" the man on the right asked.

"I'm going to come back from the dead," Jesus said.

The man clearly thought he was dying next to a man who had gone insane. "Well, before you do that," the man said, "would you put in a good word for me . . . I've not led a good life and I . . . "

Jesus looked at the man and his breathing was becoming shallow, but he managed to say, "I tell you this, my friend, this day you will be with me in Paradise." Although in incredible pain, the man smiled at Jesus—he could feel the truth in his words.

"Thank you," he said. "Thank God for you."

At that point, Jesus said to both men, "Your pain is as naught."

And in that same instant, the pain instantly went out from both men. They both wept. We were all weeping.

As he hung from the cross, it was as if he let everyone know that he loved us—completely. Although we did not, at that time understand the crucifixion (but we would in short order), what further confounded us was that he was in good humor. I tell you my Master was shining like a star and in that moment I felt him touching my spirit. I knew he could see all my failings, all of my shortcomings, my sins, and he loved me and forgave me for everything.

Oh . . . the grace . . . oh . . . the deliverance . . .

"Weep not for me," the Master said. "For I promise you, if you gather together in the upper room where we dined at the last supper, I will return to you in three days. Do . . . not . . . weep . . . for . . . me . . . ."

Speaking was getting more difficult—as was his breathing. He cried out in a loud voice, "My God, why hast thou forsaken me?"

Immediately, the Master's mother grabbed a hold of us as if she would collapse and then she said, "That was his body calling out to his soul. His soul and spirit are leaving the body—even now—"

With that, he looked at each one of us, and I could tell the Master was bestowing a blessing upon each of us and then he looked at his persecutors and said:

"Forgive them Father, for they know not what they do . . . I commend my spirit from whence it came.

"It is finished." With a breath and sigh, it was over. The Master's head dropped forward and suddenly there was a great quaking of the earth, and the bright sun was suddenly darkened. People began to scream and run. We all stayed, with our arms around each other.

"Behold," the Master's mother said, "His spirit is blotting out the sun. My son is suspended between the earth and sky. He is free."

9

Finding the Tomb Empty

When I heard the Mother of Jesus say, "Behold, my son is suspended between the earth and sky," I looked upward . . . and I cannot describe accurately what I saw except the out-line of a glorious figure—I knew it was the Master—but I could not believe that I had been blessed with the same vi-sion as Mary. Indeed, his countenance was so brilliant, so illumined, that as he hovered between the earth and sky, the sun was literally blotted out. I looked to Mary and she was swaying on her feet and then she dropped to her knees.

"God, grant me the understanding of all of these things," Mary said. "I have followed you to the death of my son . . . and I need the faith, the grace, to be strong for others to come. Grant this to me, O Lord, and take care of my son—and let this not be the end."

I helped Mary to her feet. Both of us, with John, had tears

streaming down our faces. I was horrified to see that the Roman soldiers were using iron bars to break the legs of the men who were on the left and right side of Jesus—for they were still alive. It was now the Sabbath and they were ordered by Pilate to put them out of their misery. When they came to Jesus, I stood in front of the cross and I said to the Roman guard who sought to break his legs:

"Let it be said this day that this man has been killed without a cause. You have killed an innocent man and his blood is on your hands. See how the earth quakes, see how the sun is clouded over. Fools! You have put to death the Son of God! You will not break one bone of this man's body—you will have to kill me first. The Master has already gone on to the next world. There is no need for you here. Go your way."

As I stood there, no fear was in me. I felt I was protecting the man I loved. At once, however, there was a spear thrown, and it pierced the side of the Master. I was horrified—blood and water gushed forth from his wounds and Mary, the Master's mother, covered her face.

"Damn you!" I cried. "Damn all of you who have seen fit to put this man to death, and for what crime? For Love. Love! He taught us love and healed the sick, the lame, the blind, and mark my words, your souls will be in peril for what you have done this day! You, the dogs of Pilate and Herod—if you knew who you have nailed to this tree you would be on your knees, begging for forgiveness, hiding your faces from the light of this day!" I felt the hands of a Roman guard who tried to silence me, roughly handling me. I wrenched myself free. I looked at him and said, "You may spill my blood—and I would rejoice that it may mingle with the blood of this man—the Messiah! It will be said of this man that he died without a cause—he was murdered without sin. But in his death he will make all alive again. I tell you I was raised from a death not in separation of body—but a worse, far worse state—a separateness of my soul. And he, the lowly Nazarene—gave me life when you saw fit to have me die in a pit of stones. May he, the Messiah, whom you deem criminal, forgive you. This eventide shall find you comfortless—yea, in three days you shall be afraid for your very souls—for as Lazarus, the Master shall rise again. Neither your soldiery, nor all the powers in Rome may keep him in the bonds of death."

The anger within me was the only way I could deal with the grief I was feeling. I was wild-tempered and dangerous. If any Roman would have raised a hand to quiet me, I would have ripped him to shreds. They must have seen this in my eyes for the Romans backed away from me, from Mary, the holy women, and John.

Suddenly the words of the Master came back to me—the words he said to his Mother and to John before he died. There was pain in his eyes—pain—because his mother had to witness the death of her son. And he said:

"My mother dearest, I know you long to be in Paradise with me this day, but the Father has need of you until your time is fulfilled. But, Mother, I shall be with you—this I cannot explain now, but you will understand soon." His breathing was becoming labored and I could tell it took every ounce of his being to speak to us. The Master looked to John and said, "Your years shall outnumber the other Disciples by many, John, for there is much I have yet to tell you. As I have loved you, love my Mother in the same measure. For the sun shall rise and set in your presence when you are together. Bear the dark days with her as well as the days of light. The others shall speak of betrayal more than of the hope the Father gave me to give to you—more than the hope that the Father manifested through me. They shall try to seek vengeance upon my persecutors, but I say unto you, vengeance is the Lord's, and the Lord's alone. He who forgives his adversary covers a multitude of sins. I forgive my persecutors—for if they had known the Father, they would not have done this to me. They are to be pitied, not condemned.

"John, it is but by the Father's will that I speak these words to you, for I am beyond words. Hear Him:

"After my Mother joins me—you shall be banished, but not harmed. You will be late in years, my beloved Disciple, and many will the days be that you shall be alone. Retire oft to the stillness within and listen for the call of my voice. Others shall build places of worship in my name. They shall raise monuments of gold and believe that they worship me there. But I tell you before the day passes, I will not be among the pillars of stone, nor among the raised altars. I shall be within the hearts and minds of those who *love*. And if they come together in such places to celebrate love, in my name, then I shall be there—my spirit shall be with them all. I will be in the stillness in the heart of hearts—and those who will seek me will find me in their own places of silence. Call for me, and I will come quickly.

"Mother, the Father has seen to your hour of pain that you would not be alone. Lean upon John when the days weigh heavily upon you, Mother. He shall comfort you in the earth as I shall comfort you in Spirit. Rejoice, my Mother—for it is fulfilled—you shall be called blessed above all women. Future generations will draw upon your pillar of strength. You and I, Mother, as we were one in the beginning, we shall be joined together again—even as we *are* one now. My love for you spans from the dawn of time until the end of the earth and through eternity. Without you, mankind would not know the Father, and His love for all walks of life. As you brought me into this world—so I shall be there to welcome you to the life eternal when your time comes. Even as I called you when the morning stars sang together, and proclaimed our first coming. Stand fast in my promise that I shall not leave you alone nor comfortless—I am with you, even unto the end."

I heard the Master's voice as I wrote those words—but it was not given for me to write until now. I am grateful the Master has given me the memory. Mary and John and I held onto each other and when Jesus reached the end, we all fell to our knees. After the passing of the earth-quake and the crowds fleeing in terror and confusion, John and some of the Romans helped take the lifeless body of Jesus down from the cross. A woman came up, Sophie, and she bathed the face of the Master and wiped the blood from his forehead, removing the cruel crown of thorns the Romans had placed upon his head. A dear man and close follower of the Master named Joseph asked that he be given the body of Jesus, for he had prepared a beautiful tomb for him. His wish was granted. The Roman guards were restless and I could see in their eyes that they wanted to be anywhere else but there.

"You will not be held accountable for what you have done," I said to them. "You merely followed orders. But for those who took pleasure in the death of our Lord—God help them."

With that, we carried the body of Jesus outside the Jerusalem walls—we would not have him buried in the place of his crucifixion. And what Joseph said of the tomb was true—it was beautiful. Many of the holy women brought spices and we prepared the body of Jesus for his burial. I could not stop the tears, nor could the holy women who aided us. I kissed the Master on the forehead and said, "I pray I will see you again, my beloved." For the first time, Mary spoke.

"You will see him again, Mary," she said. "You will." And there was a smile upon her face. This was not the face of a mother bereaved—but a woman who was like the mother earth herself. She was a power and a strength that I have been privileged to know. Such is a gift I shall always hold close to my heart.

We laid the Master in the beautiful tomb, and wrapped him in a beautiful linen cloth. We all held hands over the Master's body, and Mary, his mother, offered up this prayer:

"Father, you have given me a great gift—I was there when this beautiful spirit came into the world, and I was there when he departed this world. Let all that has been written be fulfilled. Imbue my son with the powers from On High, so that He may show the world what is possible, through your guiding Benevolent Spirit. And keep watch over all those gathered here and keep them safe. In the name of the Father–Mother–God, we pray."

As we left the tomb, there was a giant stone that was to be rolled in front of it. We saw that Pilate had soldiers posted around the Master's tomb.

"Would you roll the stone to cover the tomb?" I asked. A young Roman soldier came forward and said, "Yes, my lady, we will see to it." And it took four strong men to move the stone in front of the tomb.

It was then that I went with Mary to the home of John. She walked slowly and leaned upon him. We were silent as we walked—and in that silence I could feel the Master's presence with us. It was more real than anything I have ever felt. I did not feel grief–stricken, or sad. I felt an exhilaration I cannot explain. Somehow I knew the Master lived. Somewhere, beyond time and space, I knew he lived.

That night we dined and reminisced about all that we remembered of Jesus. I told the story of the only time I ever saw him angry, and that was when they were offering blood sacrifice at the temple. With a rope in one hand and chair in the other, he cleared the money–changers from their places and in a voice that was so loud and powerful he said,

"O, you hypocrites! You have turned my father's house into a den of thieves!"

Mary, his mother, remarked, "Isn't it passing strange that not one person tried to stop him? He was outnumbered by many, many men—and yet no one made a move to stop him. He let loose all the birds from their cages and all the animals that were being offered up for sacrifice. He looked at all of the people who were making a profit from their sacrifices and my son said, 'My Father desires there to be mercy, not sacrifice!'"

Many of the Disciples came into John's home that night and they fell before Mary, and she loved them all. She gave them words of comfort and said not to lose faith or hope—that it was not over yet. I could see in the eyes of the Disciples that they did not understand. In my heart, although I did not say it, I believed I would see the Master again, in this world.

Andrew told Mary that Judas had hung himself from a tree outside of Jerusalem. Mary even had compassion upon him. "Oh, that poor lost soul—if he had only waited a few more days."

"What do you mean, Mary?" Peter asked.

"I cannot speak of these things now, Peter," Mary said. "Just keep the faith and do not lose sight of what my son taught, 'Tear this temple down and in three days I will rebuild it.'"

I could see the confusion in Peter's eyes and in the eyes of many around the table. Mary knew what the rest of us did not. Her son would come back from the dead. Though he had told this in a seeming parable, he spoke in literal terms. But no one understood. Oh, I prayed that she was right! I kept this silent within my heart and uttered not a word.

I visited the tomb of Jesus every day and laid flowers outside. In my mind I conversed with him as I always did—and it seems strange, but I felt he was speaking back to me. I know how irrational that sounds, but everywhere I went, I could feel the Master's presence. I stayed with Mary for several days, and she paced the floors, looking out of her window that faced east. The parade of people who came to console her were many. Many of the Disciples came to Mary, asking her questions, wanting to know if everything was lost.

"In three days," Mary said, "you shall know the truth." To so many people she said this and they left with confused looks on their faces.

On the third day, I visited the tomb and immediately I knew something was wrong. The huge stone was rolled away. I looked within the tomb and it was empty! At that time, my mind was overwrought by the greatest sense of loss—for I feared that that someone had taken the body of the Master away. Pilate's guards were missing—they were not to be seen anywhere. The only person I found was a gardener, who was working outside of the tomb, planting roses. His back was to me and I couldn't see his face.

I sat down on a rock and I wept. The tears came and I had forgotten the words of Mary—I had forgotten the words of the Master himself who proclaimed that death would have no power over him. I was a woman bereft—lost and alone.

"Woman, why do you weep?" the man said. His back was still turned towards me.

"Sir, someone has taken the body of my Lord. My beloved. Have you seen anyone come here? I am so—"

At that moment, the man stood from his gardening duties, and turned to face me. Suddenly I could not breathe. It was *him*. Jesus. In the flesh.

"Mary." That was all he said, with all the love in his voice that I remembered from my many days with him.

When I found the words to speak, I could only utter, "Oh my God! Oh my Lord and my God!" And I ran to him.

There was a twinkle in his eye and a smile upon his lips. Gone were the bruises and the lashings upon his face and his arms. But he stepped back from me as I ran to him.

"Do not touch me as yet, Mary," the Master said. "For I am not yet finished and have not yet ascended to the Father. This body that you see is one that through the Holy Spirit has formed so you could recognize me. But if you touch me, you will be harmed in great measure—for the vibrations are yet too strong for you to touch me. But rejoice, my beloved, for death has been overcome. Go now, into Jerusalem, and tell the Disciples that I have risen from the grave. They may believe, or they may not. But make haste."

"I love you, Master," I said.

With that brilliant smile that I knew so well, he illumined my soul—

for he smiled and winked at me and said, "Why, Mary, I love you, too. Go now. For I have work to do in the other worlds. Tell the Disciples to go to the upper chamber where we had the feast before the crucifixion—in three days—I will meet with them there."

Oh! How I ran. On the way, I met Peter, James, John, and Andrew.

"I have seen him," I said.

"Who?" Peter asked in a demanding voice.

"I have seen the Master. He has arisen from the grave!"

John took me in his arms and held me as I wept with tears of joy.

"Woman, have you partaken of some strange wine?" Peter asked.

"Peter," I said. "Did you not hear the Master's words to all of us? 'Tear this temple down and I will rebuild it in three days.' He wasn't speaking about a *physical* temple. He was speaking of the temple of the body, where the soul resides! I tell you, on my honor, on all that I hold dear, that I *have seen him! The Master lives!"*

Before I gave him a chance to speak, I held up my hand to him: "Silence!" I said. "He said we were to gather in the upper chamber in three days. Now I must go and find Mary. Go tell the other Disciples and friends of the Master the message I have been charged to give you. And make haste."

I ran as fast as my feet could carry me and arrived at the threshold of Mary's home. She met me at the door with tears in her eyes.

"Mary, Mother . . . I . . . I have seen your son—and he lives," I said.

"Oh, Mary," she said. "Last night I had a dream in which my son came to me. And he crossed the threshold of my bedroom and stood before me and said, 'All is well, Mother. All is well.' I will send word to you through my beloved messenger in the morning.' And here you are!"

Mary held me fast and we wept together. "He loved you above all women," Mary said. "It was ordained that he would come to you first— and come to me in a dream. Come let us make haste to his tomb." Many of the women who were tending to Mary came with us. When we arrived at the tomb, a great light emanated from within. There I met Peter, John, James, and the other Disciples. They saw the Master's clothes folded up and laid in a corner. Behold, I was astonished and awed to see that two angels sat within the tomb. "Why do you seek the living among the dead," they asked. At first I was sore afraid. "Peace! Peace be unto all of you! For the Master Jesus is now unlocking the doors of the lower realms and setting the souls free. Jesus is descending unto the depths of hell, and traveling to the highest realms of heaven, carrying with him many souls. Go now and he will meet with you in the Upper Chamber. Tell all whom you meet that Jesus, the Master, is the first to overcome death, and he will meet with you again."

As we departed the tomb, Mary, Jesus' mother, laid her head upon the shoulder of John. "I knew it was not over. I knew that he who came from my womb was come into the world to show the world that what God has ordained, not even death can stop. Let us all rejoice."

10

I Am with You Always

I, Mary of Magdalene, bore witness to the resurrection from the dead of our Lord, Jesus, the living Christ, the living embodiment of God's love in activity. How many times did the Master tell us—and all who would listen, that Christ dwells in the heart of every man, every woman—everyone? Whether they believe or not, this eternal spark of God is hidden within the heart of all.

Throughout these writings I have called Jesus "the Master," because he was the first man—the first human being—who showed us the possibilities of what could be done—miraculous things, when the human mind aligns itself perfectly with the Unseen God, the Creator of all.

Before the Master came and dwelt among us, people worshipped gods. They once knew but had forgotten that the day would arrive when God—the All—the Creator of Heaven and earth, would come to earth, and dwell as one of us. I did not know or understand the full impact of Jesus' life and his death until he came back in the glorified body. I did not know that what brought the Master back to life was the essence of *love*. He loved even those who despitefully used him—the ones who crucified him—and forgave them. This act, combined with his love for all walks of life that he manifested in his ministry, and all the training he received during his lifetime enabled the human man to be the glorified man—and he broke the shackles of death. And that my beloved Master would choose me to show himself to first after his death and burial . . . well . . . this is a gift that is too vast for words.

When we—the Disciples, the holy women, and the Mother of Jesus— gathered in the upper room as the Master instructed, there were not a few who refused to believe my communication with the Master. I was the first to arrive in the same room in which we had the sacred Supper, and then slowly the Disciples arrived. I learned later that the Master had appeared also to some of the Disciples, but not all of them. I found myself arguing with those who did not believe I had seen the Master— particularly Matthew and Thomas. I could see in their eyes they wanted to believe I had seen him, but their rational minds could not grasp the truth of what I had seen and heard.

"Why would the Master appear to *you*, Mary?" Thomas asked. "You can see my dilemma, I am sure. I simply cannot believe that you saw the Master alive again. We traveled with him longer than you did." Thomas was not trying to be unkind, but I found myself angry at him—and the others who disbelieved.

"Did you not see the Master raise my brother, Lazarus, from the dead?" I asked. "Were you not present when he broke seven loaves of bread and fishes and—before our very eyes—created enough food to feed thousands of people? Did you not see him do this twice?"

Thomas tried to dismiss me. "Yes, Mary, I saw those things, but—"

I held my hand up before his face and silenced him. "Did you not witness the Master saving my own life? And he gave me a new life? I was dead, my brothers, my sisters, and he gave me life . . . a new life. The Master himself told you that he would rise from the dead, but you thought he spoke in parables. I did not understand until I saw him—as you too shall see him. How can you look upon me as a mad woman—beset by grief that I conjured a false vision? That it was only in my mind that I saw him and that he spoke to me?"

"I will believe, Mary," Thomas said, "When I can put my hands forth, and touch the wounds in his hands, and his side where the spear pierced him. Only then will I believe."

John spoke in my defense and said that he had been in a fishing boat and saw the Master upon the shore. At first he did not recognize him, but after they had prepared a hot meal, he looked deep into the eyes of a man he deemed a stranger in their midst and saw that it was Jesus.

Thomas shook his head. I vowed to keep my patience—for I could feel that the Master was imminently near.

"He appeared to me," I said, simply.

"And to me."

All who were in the room turned toward the voice they heard at the door and there was Mary, the blessed mother of Jesus. "It was no dream," she said, "no vision—but my son who came to me in the flesh." Upon her face was an expression of complete serenity.

"All Mary of Magdalene has told you is true," she said.

"Forgive me, Mary," Thomas said to the Master's mother and to me. "I only—"

"No need for forgiveness," the blessed mother said. "But Mary is right—you were witness to all the miracles my son performed. He is the one sent among us as the Messiah." All bowed before her—for there was a most beautiful blue light surrounding her—emanating from her. I have never seen such a beautiful vision in my life. Surprising us all, Thomas said, "The Master may have appeared to you, Blessed Mother, and to you Lady Magdalene—but . . . " I could see that he was choking back tears. " . . . but I left him. I ran away in the hour of his greatest need in the Garden—and for that—I don't believe I shall see him . . . I feel like I've betrayed your son, Mary and . . . " Mary went to Thomas as the tears spilled over his cheeks. She embraced him as a Mother would embrace a son.

"Thomas, Thomas, remember what I told you? That in order for the legacy to live on, you *had* to run away. My son had legions of angels at his side. You could not see it but I saw my son smile even when the light of death was bright in his eyes. He did not suffer as you may think he did. I know. I witnessed it. And if I, his mother, can be at peace with all that has happened, so can you."

She held Thomas and he wept. And all the Disciples and women surrounded Thomas, praying for him and blessing him. The Disciples who once did not believe said, "Forgive us for not believing . . . you are not alone, Thomas."

In the corner of the room I could see that something was happening. It was as if there was a light that was coming out of the very stones of the upper room walls themselves. I wrapped the veil around me and suddenly I knew what the Light was. I should say I knew *who the Light was*. Suddenly the entire room was filled with light. It didn't seem to come from one area, but the entire room began to become brighter, more defined. All the chattering stopped and discussion stopped. Thomas said, "What is it? What is happening?"

I looked at Mary, and her hand was at her heart. Her head was thrown back, as if she were experiencing some ecstatic vision. The vibrant blue that surrounded her became more intense. In a hushed whisper, she answered Thomas.

"He is near. He is coming—as he promised. My beloved son."

In the next moment there was a sound that we all heard—it was like the whispering of angels, or some celestial music. Peter dropped to his knees, as did all the Disciples and the holy women.

Suddenly all of the light that had filled the room was focused into the corner of the room where I first saw and felt it. The corner of the room became brighter and brighter until the outline of the Master appeared. Jude, James, and Ruth, the children of Mary were also present and they too dropped to their knees. Peter let out a gasp and made a strangled sort of noise and fell to the floor. He was lying face down upon the floor—he would not look into the corner. Out of that swirling vortex of sound and light, he, the Master, appeared. I shall never forget how he took on human form. It was as if he had formed the human body from the very elements of the room itself. At first, there was only an outline of a body. Then I could see the unmistakable countenance of the Master's beautiful face, his close-cropped beard, and then his full stature emerged from that light. But the light never dimmed behind him. It seemed to surround him from behind. He took a step forward into the room and everyone—except the Master's Mother and myself, gasped and fell to the floor weeping when they saw that it was him, our Beloved.

The smile upon his face was bright as he looked around the room at all of us.

"My son!" Mary cried, and ran to him. He opened his arms and received her embrace. "My blessed mother," the Master said. Upon hearing his voice—a voice that just days earlier I never thought I would hear again—I began to weep.

The Master held his mother for a long time and then I walked over to him.

"Lady Mary Magdalene," He said.

"My Lord and my Master," I said, as I wrapped my arms around his shoulders. This was no ghostly image, no phantom—Jesus was flesh and blood, standing before us all. "I dreamed of this day," I said, tears spilling over my cheeks and onto his robe—I found it difficult to speak. "My beloved who was once dead is alive again," I whispered. He held me tightly. "All is well, Mary, all is well. It is accomplished. Death has been conquered."

I released myself from his embrace and looked into those blue-gray eyes. He smiled at me. I could not think of anything else to say, I was so overwhelmed with joy. He then in turn embraced his brothers and sisters. When he came to Ruth I heard her say, "I cannot believe this—as Mary said, my brother who was dead is alive again." He took her into his arms and he swirled her around in a circle.

"It is I," the Master said, not without the familiar sense of humor we had come to love so well. "Remember what I said: What God has ordained, no man may halt nor hinder." The Disciples and the accompanying women were all lying upon the floor, weeping, afraid it seemed, to raise their faces to him. It was Mary who broke the spell.

"Arise! All of you," she said, "And behold the glory of God." Everyone stood except Thomas and Peter, who lay weeping upon the floor. In the most tender and gentle way, the Master moved through the crowd and knelt beside Thomas and Peter.

"Thomas," the Master said, "Arise." He was visibly shaking as he slowly stood up and faced the Master. When Thomas saw that it truly was the Master, he wept again. "Forgive me, Master—I—I" he too had difficulty finding words to say. "Give me your hand" the Master said. Thomas held out his shaking hand. "Do you feel the wounds upon my left and right hands?" Jesus placed Thomas' hand upon the places upon his wrists where the nails were driven. They were not seeping, but it was clear the wounds were still there. Thomas looked into his eyes, searching and finding the forgiveness he sought. "Now," the Master said, "place your hand upon my side and feel the place where the spear pierced me." The Master placed Thomas' hand upon his abdomen firmly. "Can you feel that?"

"Yes, Master," Thomas said.

"You are blessed because you have seen and believed. But blessed shall be those who do not see, but believe." Then the Master turned his attention to Peter who still lay upon the floor.

"Get up, my friend," Jesus said.

"I cannot," Peter said, choking out the words.

"Why?" the Master asked.

"Because I betrayed you—I denied that I even knew you—three times, just as you said I would. I cannot face what I have done to you."

"Peter," Jesus said, in a most compassionate voice, "I told you those things so that you would *do just that*. Had you not denied me, they would have killed you. You followed my mother's direction. The legacy would have died with you had you admitted you were one of my Disciples. Come now, and arise and face me. You can no longer deny that I have chosen you."

Upon hearing those words, Peter stood before the Master. He looked into his eyes and then threw his arms around his shoulders and embraced him. "Peter," the Master said, "You are the rock upon which I shall build my church. You must be strong in the days to come. All of you must be strong in the days to come. Arise, all of you—this is a time for celebration!"

The Master's voice seemed to take on a booming tone, that made everyone arise, and suddenly it was a celebration. Everyone came to him—asking his forgiveness for not believing, for not understanding what was meant when he said, "Tear this temple down, and I shall rebuild it in three days."

He hugged and laughed with all those present that he had known and loved before his trial. And his laughter filled the room. It seemed to me that the ceiling in that upper room was gone—and I could see angels and beings of light coming and going—singing praises from on high. The most beautiful music I've ever heard!

The Master showed us all his wounds. His mother came forth and kissed his hands, his wrists, and held his hands to her heart. "My son, my son," she said. "How is it that you are here with us, in flesh and blood?"

And Jesus spoke. His message reached our hearts this time, and not just our ears. "The paths of carnal life do not run up the mountain towards the top—they run around the mount of life. Around and around and the soul goes but no higher. The Father–Mother–God, from my earliest learning under the masters of the East, taught me that all people can reach God, but one must give up the carnal life and go straight to the upper gate of consciousness. All of my life was spent going straight to the summit of God. All of you, in your ascent to the summit where God dwells—in consciousness—within your own selves, will be tempted and tried. You shall cross the paths of carnal life on the way through the straight and narrow gate that leads to life everlasting, but tread not the side roads, for they will take you around and around.

"This is the mystery of the cross," the Master added. "For the earth pulls man this way (he stretched his arms out in a horizontal way), and the path to the highest mount where God and man are one in consciousness moves this way. (The Master knelt down upon the floor and slowly raised his arms upward, until he looked like a straight, brilliant line—pointing to the heavens and down to the earth.) All souls reach the crossroads in life where they are pulled from side to side by the carnal life—and yet ever is the call within to go upwards to the straight and narrow path. In your prayer and meditations, pray for strength and guidance that you will ascend to the highest summit and not be tempted by the snares of the carnal world. For this reason, dear Mother," he looked to Mary, "did I go into the wilderness for forty days and forty nights. I had to face the ultimate challenge and be tempted in ways I cannot describe by the prince of this world—Satan. In that test, I was promised every pleasure the earth could offer. I was offered power over all nations and all people by the Dark One. I stayed close to the Father in those times and prayed for strength, for my carnal self had not yet died—until I left the desert and returned to be among you again. It was a test. And then I was again tested in the Garden of Gethsemane. I knew that all had been accomplished but I feared the pangs of death." At this, the Master actually laughed. "Death is nothing but a threshold—a crossing of a bridge to higher consciousness. In allowing myself to be captured and crucified, I became the cross, so that I could become the Way, the Truth, and the Life everlasting. Now, all souls can call upon me, for my soul is at one with the Triune God—and I am the first of many who will overcome death. Even now, I remember not the pain of my death, my passing from this world. I know that it happened, and I know it appeared brutal to all of you. But, my friends, God is a mystery, a glorious mystery, and He enabled me to pass through death with my soul unscathed.

"This is how you and all people must bear your cross. Bear it not with long-facedness and sorrow, but with laughter and joy. Be thankful for the things that beset you, that you must work through—for all of you are wounded healers. If you were not wounded, you would not seek to aid, to heal, others. You would have no compassion in your hearts if you did not have your own cross to bear. I do not mean that you must be crucified as I was, no, but in heart and Spirit you shall be tried, and there will be times where it will *feel as if you were being crucified.* Then, in those hours, call upon me and I will be with you. Even as I called to God in the Garden, "My God, my God, be thou near unto me, just now!" This prayer enabled me to lay aside my physical life so that I could take it up again.

"In your walk through life, my friends, know that you cannot bear another person's cross—but you can encourage the discouraged, bring hope to those who are lost in despair, give strength to the weary. For though the earth life is not easy, it is in passing through all experiences, as I did—experiences of both shadow and light—that the soul may purge itself from everything that stands in the way of the soul's ascent to the Mount where the soul and God are one. Faint not when trouble comes—

for everyone must bear their own cross and those who endure to the end shall wear the crown of eternal life."

To me, it was as if we were sitting on a hillside, as we did so many times before, sitting at the Master's feet, and listening to his teachings. I had to remind myself that he indeed had died and had resurrected. He was more vibrant, more powerful, more than he had ever been during his earthly life. Truly, not only had he *not* lost his life, he had found it, and in abundance. My heart leapt within me for joy at hearing his voice again.

"Each day," the Master said, "envision your life as a climb up to the Summit of God—and look not back to the shadows of the past. Face the light and the shadows of earthly concerns shall fall far behind. I am a living testament to this truth. For though I was tried, convicted falsely, accused of ridiculous crimes, I looked upon my persecutors as unruly children who were acting out of fear. Even at their worst, I prayed to see them as God saw them—as loving beings who had gone astray. Their lessons to be learned will be difficult—for that which is meted to others must be met again in self. In some future time, or in the present, everything returns to us—the good and the bad. This is a law—the law of cause and effect. So set your path to bring forth only positive causes for all mankind, and you will reap positive effects in life.

"But know, my friends—and you *are* my friends—not my servants. You are not beneath me, but are equal with me—remember you are Christ *becoming*. You are gods in the making. Look not back upon your shortcomings or your weaknesses, neither condemn yourself or others but look forward. And you too will one day attain the pearl at great price. You will be pearls even though now you may see yourself as a grain of sand!" With that, he laughed—a hearty laugh.

"I shall return to you in a little while, but now it must needs be that I show myself to those who do not believe in me and what is possible. I must go forth and show those who considered me an enemy, that I am *not* the enemy."

"You mean that you are going to see Pilate and the High Priests?" I asked.

The Master smiled. "Yes, my dear one, I will visit them and many others. I will go throughout the world and show myself to those who are attuned to me, those who believe that the time has arrived when death shall be overcome. For now, I bid you farewell, but I shall return to you . . . for a little while. Now go forth and tell others you have seen me, and that I live. And if I live, they shall have eternal life also. Some will believe, many will believe—but many will not believe—do not worry. Think of it as scattering seeds. Some seeds fall upon stony ground and are picked up by the birds. Other seeds fall upon fertile ground and grow into mighty trees. This is the task I ask you to do for me. In love, go forth—and be not afraid. And there are some here who will not escape the fate that I have just passed through. Remember, even in the darkest hour, I shall be with you. Call my name, and I will be with you in Spirit, in Mind, and in Body. So fear not."

After saying these words, the Master blessed all of us in the room, and placed his hands upon the heads of all. And as he did, he told us that during the three days that his body lay within the tomb, that he had not only ascended into the heavens, but had gone to the farthest reaches of the netherworlds—places some call hell—where those souls abide who do not believe themselves worthy to be in the presence of God for one reason or another. Jesus went in Spirit to these places and opened the prison doors of their minds and said, "Follow me," and many, many souls followed the Master into the heavens. In a dream I saw Judas, who was alone in a dark place. I could see him sitting beneath the tree where he hanged himself. In the dream, Jesus took Judas by the hand and Judas stood up, not comprehending at first what was happening. The Master told him that without him, the Resurrection could not have happened. Before that dream I thought, *if only Judas had held on a little bit longer—just a few short days.* But in my dream, I saw him being led to the realms of Light, the realms of God, holding onto the Master's arm, weeping. Jesus had forgiven his betrayer. And I thought, *could I not do the same?* Many of the so-called followers of the Master condemn Judas and they do not look at the whole situation.

The Master dwelt with us for many days, and indeed, he went around the world to sacred places in India, Persia, Tibet, and Egypt, where the Sacred Brotherhoods had a chair or a throne that was surrounded by a veil and was reserved for the first person to overcome death. Jesus told me, during the time he dwelt among us that he had proclaimed that "It is finished. Praise God everlasting—for what I have done, all people shall do." So the word was spread throughout the world of what Jesus had done. For his having overcome death and the grave, and then resurrected, the world itself was changed.

The hardest part for me was when he told me and the others that he had to go to the Father–Mother–God, and that one day, he would come again and receive all people unto himself.

"You mean I shall not see you anymore?" I asked.

Jesus took me by the hand. "I shall never leave you, Mary. My spirit, the Holy Spirit, shall be with you always. And I shall appear to many people in dreams and visions—and so will my Mother when her time comes to leave this world. Do not be sad, Mary, for I will wait for you and will be with you."

"But to never touch your face, or look into the blue of your eyes," I said, weeping. "I am afraid I shall return to my old life if I do not see you."

Jesus smiled that smile I knew so well. "You are long past that temptation, Mary. In the hours of longing, be it in the night or in the day, call upon me and I shall hear and answer you."

"So we shall not be apart?" I asked. I felt childish in asking the Master such things, but remember my friends, I was in love—a love that was greatest among any love I had ever known. How easy would it be for you to let go of the one you loved the most?

"No, Mary, we shall not be apart," the Master said. "Now, come with me. Many are waiting for us. And as I always dreamed—he walked with me, arm in arm up a steep hillside near the Mount of Olives. There were hundreds of people there, cheering as they saw him. Jesus paused awhile with the crowd in an exceedingly cool and lovely spot covered with long beautiful grass. The multitude that surrounded him was so great, I could no longer count them. Jesus spoke to them a very long time, like one who is about the business of closing his discourse and coming to a conclusion.

He never released my arm until he gave his final pronouncement.

Jesus spoke: "In sensing your light which is God, your adversaries only know to defend their dark, fearful selves. They attack out of fear, unknowing and are shackled by demons of guilt, shame, and self-loathing. Keep distant from these cowardly attacks—and forgive them because they do not know that the Light is not their enemy. My Father loves these unruly ones—for they are like damaged and hurt children—who lost their way in the shadowlands. Even if they, in their cowardice and fear seek to silence you, stifle you, even kill you—justifying themselves to be doing a service to God by slaying you—do not respond in kind. Michael and his protectorate angels and I shall free you from their ignorant and hateful confines. But even Holy Michael cannot wield his benevolent sword—he cannot protect you with his righteous shield if you choose to hate. Even the powers and desire of God cannot intervene for you unless you—in your heart and in My spirit—love the dark ones as a parent loves a difficult child.

"Soon—when my followers learn and manifest this mystic secret of Love as the Force which conquers the evil—Michael shall be empowered to remove the dark ones from the New Earth and their domain will be in another world where they will learn love in a hard, but meaningful way. Then, you, I, all who were persecuted for speaking of the Light—the ones who were silenced because of Love—all will return in that great rebirth, and the earth shall be filled with the legions of benevolent warriors of the heart called the *Meek Ones*. The Meek Ones are my children, Mary's children, and Disciples of Michael—who taught them the true and just warrior uses Love as its battle-ax. The Meek shall come—and then, my Mother, in all her splendor shall appear in the four corners of the earth, giving signs in many places, and giving messages. And the Meeks will be brought together by her—in preparation for their inheritance of the New Earth. They will conquer every adversary. They will be tried as I was. They shall pass through the darkness and when all hope seems gone, the Meek Ones will look up and my voice will awaken them through signs and wonders—and all will remember they are of the Holy Order of the Divine Father-Mother-God.

"And in that day the very powers in earth which have ruled with force and tyranny and oppression shall crumble—by their *own* sword. And the great illusion shall protect the dark ones no more. Their selfish reign of countless millennia shall end. They—not my Meek Ones—shall wail and gnash their teeth—their self-willed refusal to love will be heard in a terrible thunder. In that day, know my Father and Michael are taking these hurt ones away and they will not be hurt or punished. But their souls will be *re-mastered* in another world, where they will learn to trust again. Gabriel shall remold their guilt-ridden spirits to remember the darkness no more. Remember, even the ones who are the most evil are only one step from my light. Know this—remember this, my little ones. Show love to them, but *do not* be subservient nor do their biddings in these last days.

"We, the warriors for Light and heart, will remove them from power. Fear not. And watch for my Mother in the clouds, in strange places—the signs will reflect her countenance—which will awaken you to remember this Covenant. Then she shall give some final teachings through your minds and hearts in visions. She will tell you how to do final preparations. My Mother is the Great Spirit who will entrust you to be my doorway. She will open you to receive my spirit—just as she opened her heart in pure love and conceived my first perfect expression as Jesus. Then, in thought, spirit, deeds, and visions, wondrous works will happen. These I cannot say to you now—but all will feel the Great Shift— unseen. And in that Divine Moment, time as the earth has known it, shall cease. And I, my brothers and sisters, shall be born through the purity of your hearts. *Your hearts* will be the avenue—in harmony with all Meek Ones in the four corners of the earth—of my Second Return— my Second Coming. Then, I shall come into the earth *through* you—and we again will be reunited in body and heart. Remember this day of Ascension for I promise to be with you always. Remember my promise, this generation shall not be complete until you gather again and I shall come even as you will see me go. This time, my loved ones, my advent into the New Earth will be witnessed by not just a few, but the masses.

"Keep the faith. I love you. Peace in Gethsemane. It is dark and hard as labor, but through this, my Passion, you will know my way and will *become* my way. Godspeed my friends. Remember me in joy and laughter and love. I am with you always. I am imminent, and I am with you always, even unto the end of the old things, and the beginning of the new."

As the Master finished his pronouncement, a great light in heaven opened up, and the Master was resplendent as a beam of white sunlight. He laid his left hand upon his breast and raised his right into the heavens and repeated, "I am with thee always . . . all days . . . " And I could feel that he was blessing the whole world. The crowd stood motionless, but many were weeping with tears of joy, and also sadness, for they knew his physical presence was leaving this world. The rays of light from above united with the glory emanating from Jesus and I saw him disappearing, dissolving as it were in the light of Heaven, vanishing as he rose. It was as if the sun had merged with the light of the Master's countenance—and I saw two angelic beings descending from Heaven and each one stood upon the right and left side of him. He looked down upon me and I wiped the tears from my face—and he smiled upon me. "I love you," the Master said to me, to the crowd, to the world. "Remember, I am with you always, even unto the end." I watched as he disappeared into the vibrant light of the heavens and then it was like a shower of light came down upon us. Oh, the splendor! Oh, the amazement! I knew, then, in my heart that indeed the Master would always be with me—closer to me than my own breath.

I and the group continued to look upwards long after Jesus had ascended into heaven and an angel appeared and spoke to the crowd.

"Why do you look heavenward, O people of Israel?" the angel asked. "Jesus, the Christ, whom you have seen taken into Heaven shall return to you even as you have seen him go. He shall dwell within your hearts and minds as long as you hold a place for him. So go now, and preach the gospel that the Master has directed. That there is no death, and that all things the Master has done, so shall all people who *love* do also. Go now and peace be with you."

I have reflected upon my life with the Master many times and it was all too brief that I walked the earth with him. But I shall never forget, though I live a thousand lifetimes and falter in a thousand more, the words that he gave to me—about love in a loveless world. Of compassion to those who move out of fear. Of honoring his memory by forgiving my enemies.

My time has come now to end this diary. It is being taken to a hiding place with other sacred writings, I have been told. I do not consider this "sacred" except that I had the opportunity to speak of the Master, and his walk through the earth. This is a privilege I do not know what I did to earn. I am grateful for him and for his words and his love more than I can say.

John has just arrived and I am being moved now from this subterranean basement to his home for a time—and then we are to sail to Gaul[1]. I feel a strange stirring within me—as if there is a light or a life within my body that I've never known. I do not know what the future holds—but I know that with the Master at my side, all will be well. Even now I can hear the echo of his words and see the smile upon his face, "I am with you always, Mary."

Always.

---

[1]France

DISCOVER HOW THE EDGAR CAYCE MATERIAL CAN HELP YOU!

The Association for Research and Enlightenment, Inc. (A.R.E.®), was founded in 1931 by Edgar Cayce. Its international headquarters are in Virginia Beach, Virginia, where thousands of visitors come year-round. Many more are helped and inspired by A.R.E.'s local activities in their own hometowns or by contact via mail (and now the Internet!) with A.R.E. headquarters.

People from all walks of life, all around the world, have discovered meaningful and life-transforming insights in the A.R.E. programs and materials, which focus on such areas as personal spirituality, holistic health, dreams, family life, finding your best vocation, reincarnation, ESP, meditation, and soul growth in small-group settings. Call us today at our toll-free number:

1-800-333-4499

or

Explore our electronic visitors center on the
Internet: **http://www.edgarcayce.org.**

We'll be happy to tell you more about how the work of the A.R.E. can help you!

A.R.E.
215 67th Street
Virginia Beach, VA 23451-2061